THE BABY-SITTERS CLUB

Jessi's Gold Medal
Ann M. Martin

AN
APPLE
PAPERBACK

SCHOLASTIC INC.
New York Toronto London Auckland Sydney

Cover art by Hodges Soileau

No part of this publication may be reproduced in whole or in part, or stored in a retrieval system, or transmitted in any form or by any means, electronic, mechanical, photocopying, recording, or otherwise, without written permission of the publisher. For information regarding permission, write to Scholastic Inc., 730 Broadway, New York, NY 10003.

ISBN 0-590-44964-8

12 11 10 9 8 7 6 5 4 3 2 1   2 3 4 5 6 7/9

Printed in the U.S.A.   40

First Scholastic printing, June 1992

*The author gratefully acknowledges
Peter Lerangis
for his help in
preparing this manuscript.*

Special thanks to
Carol Grossman
for her expertise on synchronized swimming
and for her enthusiastic help.

CHAPTER 1

"All right, ladies, *tour jeté* across ze room!" Mme Noelle called out.

Our ballet class was almost over. We were all sweating horribly. (Oops! I mean, we were *glowing*. As Madame says, "Horses sweat, gentlemen perspire, and ladies *glow!*") Was Madame going to let us do some gentle *pliés* to cool down a little? Nooo. We were going to turn-and-leap, turn-and-leap around the room. That's what *tour jetés* are. If you can do them really well, like Misha Baryshnikov (one of my heroes), you look like you're flying.

If you're an eleven-year-old girl in Mme Noelle's Tuesday afternoon ballet class in Stamford, Connecticut, you look . . . well, you look like you've had a long day.

We lined up on the left side of the studio. Mme Noelle stood by a tape recorder with her finger over the play button, and said, "Mademoiselle Romsey, please lead." (That's me.

Actually, I'm Jessica *Ramsey*, but it comes out *Romsey* in Mme Noelle's French accent.)

A loud waltz blared out of the speakers. I rounded my right arm and took a few steps to the right. Then, in a split second, here's what happened: My body spun around. My right leg lifted off the ground. My arm shot forward in an arc — and I was soaring! (Maybe not like Misha, but as close as I could get.) I did it again and again, springing into the air at each downbeat of the waltz.

When I completed a circle around the room, I could hear Madame say, "Good leeft, Mademoiselle Romsey, very gracefool — but do not let zee trailing arm droop."

"Okay," I said, only I was panting so hard it came out more like, "Kuhhh."

I was hot and grimy and I just wanted to plop onto the floor. A big fan in the corner was blowing warm, musty air across the room — definitely *not* refreshing. But here's the strange thing: I felt great. In fact, I wouldn't have minded if class had lasted another hour. Why? Because I love ballet. Even after seven years of lessons, I *still* get excited just walking into class. You know how some people seem to be "born" comedians or artists or athletes? Well, I'm a born dancer. Wait a minute, that sounds conceited. What I mean is, dancing makes me happier than anything else. Also, I have these really long legs, which "turn out" naturally (a big advantage).

I've already learned to dance on my toes (which is called *en pointe*) and I've played lead roles in a few ballets, like Swanilda in *Coppélia* and Princess Aurora in *Sleeping Beauty*. Someday I hope to be a professional ballerina, *if* I can stand the years of hard work and "dee-seepleen," Madame's favorite word (translation: *discipline*). And *that* means the rest of my life would be like this:

1. Watching what I eat. (Have you ever seen a fat ballerina?).

2. Taking as many classes a week as possible.

3. Stretching all the time, to keep my muscles limber.

4. Becoming familiar with the classical ballets I might be in someday.

Pretty tough, huh? My dad says being a ballerina is like being in the army — except in boot camp you don't wear a tutu.

My dad, by the way, has a great sense of humor. Which comes in handy whenever he has to wait for me in his car outside my dance school after a long day's work. Which is what he was doing that Tuesday of the *tour jetés*.

Madame's voice was ringing out, "On ze *beat*, on ze *beat*, on ze *beat*, on ze *beat* . . ." as Julie Mansfield leaped across the room. I

3

quickly did some stretching exercises at the *barre*, then ran to the changing room.

In seconds I was dressed in white sweatpants, pink leg warmers, and a pink-and-white sweat shirt that said "ABT," which stands for American Ballet Theater. I stuffed my sweaty (glowy?) dance clothes in my canvas bag, slung it over my shoulder, and ran out of school.

Daddy was waiting in the car, a big smile on his face. "Hi, baby," he said as I climbed in the passenger seat. "How was class?"

"Fine," I answered. "How was work?"

"Don't ask!" Daddy said, laughing. Lately we say the same thing after ballet class. It's like a ritual. The best part is Daddy's laugh, which is deep and booming. He sounds sort of like James Earl Jones, the famous actor.

Daddy drove away from the curb and headed toward the expressway. We live in Stoneybrook, which is just a few exits away. Stoneybrook's a nice place, but I didn't think so at first. We're black, and Stoneybrook is, like, ninety percent white. We used to live in Oakley, New Jersey, in a neighborhood where blacks and whites lived together and everybody got along just fine.

Stoneybrook isn't like that. When we first moved here, it was a real shock. Some people were nasty to us, just because of our skin color. The things they said and did were so prejudiced and stupid. I wanted to move back to Oakley so much. But my mom and dad always believed things would work out, and they were right.

First of all, people have gotten used to us (doesn't that sound weird?). Second of all, I became best friends with a girl named Mallory Pike. And *third* of all, Mallory and I became members of the Baby-sitters Club. (I'll tell you more about Mal and the BSC later.)

My dad mopped his forehead with a handkerchief as we pulled onto the expressway. He was sweating — I mean *perspiring* — like crazy. Even though it was still spring, it felt like midsummer. We had to drive right under a billboard advertising some soda as the "official drink of the Summer Olympics." There was a huge picture of a swimmer splashing through the water, in the middle of a stroke. She was working hard, but boy, did she look *coooool*. For a minute I thought I was crazy to like ballet. Why pound your body into a wood floor when you could plunge it into water instead?

Daddy was looking at the billboard, too. He sighed and said, "What do you say we use the air conditioner?"

"Sure!" I said. Supposedly air conditioning is bad for dancers, because it can tighten your muscles. But I have to admit, I love it on really hot days.

So we drove home comfortably, without any perspiration or glow.

Our house is on a street shaded with big maple trees. But it might as well have been the Sahara desert when we got out of the car. The hot, steamy air was almost enough to make you choke.

"Hi, Daddy! Hi, Jessi!" squealed my sister Becca from inside the front screen door. She ran outside, wearing a one-piece bathing suit with strange, multicolored designs on it. (No, not some fancy designer swimwear. Becca is eight, and she decided she could make her solid white suit look a lot better with markers.) "Can we play in the sprinkler?" she asked.

"Seee-gahh! Day-eee!"

That last voice was my little brother, Squirt. I had to laugh when I saw him running across the lawn. His teeny legs were doing about a hundred steps per second, but he was moving forward so slowly. Squirt is almost a year and a half old. He's been walking for a few months, and now he's starting to talk. For example, I'm pretty sure "Seee-gahh! Day-eee!" meant "Sprinkler, Daddy!"

My aunt Cecelia suddenly appeared at the door, holding a pair of turquoise jellies. "John

Philip, come in here and put on your sandals!" (John Philip Ramsey, Jr., is my brother's real name. But he was so puny at birth that the nurses in the hospital called him Squirt, and the nickname stuck — except with Aunt Cecelia sometimes.)

Aunt Cecelia is my dad's sister. She moved in with us to help take care of Squirt when my mom got a job. Aunt Cecelia is sometimes hard to take — and that's a *nice* thing to say, compared to the way I used to talk about her. I used to think she was a cross between the Bride of Frankenstein and Freddy Krueger's mother. When she first got here she was bossy and mean and awful. She treated Becca and me like babies, and tried to control our lives. But we "had it out" and things have gotten a lot better.

"Please! Please!" Becca was tugging at Daddy's pants leg now. "Mama says it's okay!"

"She does?" Daddy asked.

"I said it's okay if it's okay with *Daddy!*" came Mama's voice from inside. "And if Jessi doesn't mind watching you!"

"Please?" Becca repeated to Daddy, then turned to me. "You'll watch us, right?"

"Peeeez!" Squirt was now wearing his jellies and was toddling toward Daddy.

Daddy picked up Becca in one arm and Squirt in the other. "Well, I don't know," he said. Then with a wink, he added, "What do you think, big sister?"

"Well, I have a lot of homework," I replied, pretending to mean it. Poor Becca's face just sank, so I quickly added, "But I'll watch for a while."

"Yippee! Yippee!"

Daddy let Becca down, and she raced around to the back of the house. Daddy followed, carrying Squirt, and I followed them. Becca got the sprinkler out of our garage, and I helped her attach it to the garden hose. Then Daddy, Becca, and Squirt unrolled the hose into the middle of the backyard. I stayed by the faucet.

When they had set it up, Becca called out, "Ready!"

I turned the faucet on. The water shot upward, sending a cold shower over Squirt and Becca. They both started squealing wildly.

With a big smile, Daddy said, "Let's keep it to about fifteen minutes, okay? I'm going to change and then help Mama and Cecelia with dinner."

"Okay."

So there I was, sitting on a lawn chair, watching my brother and sister having the time of their lives. I thought about the summer coming up, and about how this was only the *start* of the hot weather, and about how often we'd be using the sprinkler. Then I thought about that billboard on the expressway, with the Olympic swimmer . . . and that was when the idea came to me.

A pool.

It made so much sense. Sprinklers are great, but a pool is much better. You can use it all day long, and you can exercise while you cool off. Not to mention pool parties. And besides, our backyard was the perfect size for one.

I had a feeling it would be impossible to convince my parents, until I remembered a great technique Mal had thought up. She had used it when she needed to convince her parents to let her take horseback-riding lessons — and it worked.

I decided to try my own version of it that evening at dinner.

"Great seafood casserole, Mama!" I began. This was step one — complimenting the meal and making my parents feel good.

"I'm glad you like it," Mama said. "Your dad took care of the seasoning."

"Mmmm, great seasoning," I added. "Just right for a hot day. May I have some more?" This was step two — mentioning the weather. I was working up to the climax (step three) where I'd bring up the pool.

"Thanks," Daddy said with a laugh. "You usually don't get so excited about a meal unless we're going to Pizza Express. You don't just happen to *want* something, do you, Jessi?" He looked at me with raised eyebrows.

"What?" I said.

"Just a hunch. Correct me if I'm wrong."

Step three was fizzling into thin air. I couldn't believe it. He could read my mind!

"Well . . ." I said, "I was just thinking about how hot it gets here in Stoneybrook, and how it's going to be a long summer, and we could use a place to cool off . . ."

"Sweetheart, the weather's no different here than in Oakley," Mama said.

"I know, but we have this nice big backyard, and — well, the sprinkler is great, but maybe we could get something we *all* can use. You know, like a pool."

There. I said it. Aunt Cecelia let out a huffy little laugh (typical). But Becca's eyes lit up and she exclaimed, "A *pool*! Yeah, let's get a pool!"

Squirt clapped his hands and bounced up and down, but I'm not sure he knew *why* he was doing it.

"I mean, we're going to be home most of the summer," I added quickly, "and there won't be that much for me to do besides take ballet classes and watch the Summer Olympics, and you and Dad will be able to relax in it, too, and we can teach Squirt how to swim at an early age . . ."

I looked at Mama and Daddy, and fortunately they didn't seem too shocked. "Well, believe it or not, we have talked about it," Mama said.

"Yea!" Becca yelled.

"The problem is, pools are extremely expensive," Daddy said. "Not only buying them and putting them in, but maintaining them. It's out of our reach — that is, unless you kids want to go without food or clothes for a year or so."

Daddy said that last part with a smile, but Becca looked kind of confused. "I could chip in with baby-sitting money," I suggested.

"That's sweet of you, Jessi," Mama said, "But you need that for other things. Besides, it wouldn't be nearly enough."

"Ask your boss to give you more money!" Becca suggested.

Daddy and Mama both roared with laughter. "Will you come with us when we do it?" Daddy asked.

I could smell defeat. I knew that when my parents said it was too much money, there was no hope.

"Well, it was just an idea . . ." I said, trying not to sound *too* disappointed.

11

"And a good one," Mama replied. "But you know, there is a way to have *access* to a pool all summer. What about the Stoneybrook Community pool complex?"

"They have two or three pools," Daddy said. "One of them is Olympic sized, too. And they give lessons. That's something you don't get with a backyard pool."

What a great idea. I had forgotten all about the pool complex. I knew how to swim, but not that well. Lessons would be a great project for the summer. Suddenly I felt excited again. "Could we join?" I asked.

"I don't see why not," Daddy said. "I'll call tomorrow and ask about getting a family membership."

"Goody!" Becca said.

"Gooey!" Squirt said.

"That make you feel better, sweetheart?" Mama asked.

I nodded. It wasn't *exactly* what I had in mind, but the more I thought about it, the more I liked the idea. The summer was going to be all right, after all.

CHAPTER 2

"Order!" yelled Kristy Thomas as the clock turned to 5:30.

No, I wasn't in court, or in a restaurant. I was in Claudia Kishi's bedroom on Wednesday, the day after the pool discussion. Kristy was sitting in a director's chair, wearing a visor turned backward. Claudia was seated cross-legged on her bed next to Stacey McGill and Mary Anne Spier. Dawn Schafer was sitting at Claud's desk, and Mallory Pike and I were lounging on the floor.

What were we doing? Well, for the seven of us, Wednesday at 5:30 means one thing: a Baby-sitters Club meeting. (Monday and Friday, too — also at 5:30.) I promised I'd tell you about the BSC, so here goes.

The name "Baby-sitters Club" says everything about us (almost). We're experienced baby-sitters, and we're a club of best friends. Here's how the club (actually, it's a business) works: for a half hour (till 6:00), we sit in Claudia's room and wait for phone calls from Stoneybrook parents who need sitters. Each time someone calls, we figure out who's available for the job. We try to spread the jobs among ourselves so everyone has the same amount.

It works out great for us *and* the parents. *They* only need to make one phone call to reach seven great sitters — and one of us is almost always available (we have two associate members in case the rest of us are booked up). And *we* can be sure to have a pretty steady amount of work.

By now, most of the local parents know about us. They tell their friends, and the word spreads around. But it wasn't always like that. At the beginning, the BSC used to advertise — putting fliers in schools and supermarkets, stuff like that. From time to time, we still advertise. Kristy makes us (she's the president).

Another thing Kristy makes us do is fill in the official BSC notebook. We're supposed to write up every job we go on. This is a very useful thing to do, even though we all grumble whenever Kristy reminds us about it.

What do we do between phone calls? That's where the "club" part comes in. We're all good friends, so we never run out of things to talk about. We also try to think up new projects

14

— which mostly means listening to the projects Kristy thinks of.

As you can guess, Kristy can be bossy. But her suggestions are amazing. When anyone says the word "idea," I think, "Kristy." I can't help it. You know how a dry sponge soaks up water if you put it in a puddle? That's what Kristy's brain is like. It's an idea sponge. She soaks up ideas from the air, then squeezes them out at meetings. And usually they're really good. Like the time there was a group of kids who were too young to play on a softball team. Kristy got them together and formed a team of her own. They're called "Kristy's Krushers."

Here's another example: Kid-Kits. They're simple, decorated boxes filled with stuff we scrounge up around our houses — old games, books, toys, art supplies, things like that. Doesn't sound too exciting, right? Wrong. You wouldn't believe how popular they are. Even kids with incredibly fancy toys *love* Kid-Kits. Leave it to Kristy.

Speaking of which, can you guess who thought of the idea of the Baby-sitters Club to begin with? Right. It came to Kristy a long time ago, on a day when her mom was frantically trying to get a baby-sitter. Back then, Mrs. Thomas was a single parent, raising

Kristy and her three brothers. Kristy watched her mom make phone call after phone call, and no one was available. Then, bingo! The idea sponge went to work. Why not have one central number, Kristy thought — like an agency with available baby-sitters? She started planning the Baby-sitters Club, and the rest is history.

In case you were worried, Kristy's mom isn't a single parent anymore. Let me explain. Ready to hear a real-life fairy tale? Here goes.

Once upon a time, Kristy lived with her dad and mom and her older brothers, Charlie and Sam. When she was about six, two things happened. First another brother was born (David Michael). Then Mr. Thomas decided to split. No explanations, no nothing. He just ran off to California. And divorced Mrs. Thomas, and married someone else. (Needless to say, Kristy doesn't like to talk about him, and I don't blame her.) Things got tough for awhile, but Mrs. Thomas managed to hold down a job *and* bring up four kids. Then, a few years later, she started dating this nice guy named Watson Brewer, who was also divorced and happened to have two kids of his own, Karen and Andrew. He also happened to be a millionaire and he lived in a mansion across town. Mrs. Thomas and Watson got married, the Thomases moved into the mansion, and everyone lived happily ever after.

Isn't that a romantic story? It's all true, too, especially the mansion part. It's huge! Now the Brewer/Thomas family includes Emily Michelle, adopted from Vietnam; Nannie, Kristy's grandmother; a dog; a cat; and two goldfish. Karen and Andrew live there only every other weekend, but even with them around there's *still* plenty of room in the house.

The mansion is pretty far from Claudia's house, but Charlie drives Kristy to our meetings (he's seventeen).

There's a good reason our meetings are at Claudia's. She's the only one of us who has her own phone. What's Claudia like? In many ways, the opposite of Kristy. While Kristy's super-practical, Claudia is a real artist. She can paint, sculpt, draw, and design jewelry. While Kristy's brimming with ideas, Claudia's brimming with . . . junk food! And I mean *brimming*. She has stuff hidden in every nook and cranny. Ring Dings, Milky Ways, pretzels, chips — if it's bad for you, she has it. And she loves to share it with us. (As you can guess, BSC meetings are *not* dietetic.) Another way she's different from Kristy is in *style*. Kristy's short and tomboyish, and she usually dresses in jeans or sweats with running shoes. She hardly ever wears makeup, and she lets her long brown hair hang straight. Claudia, on the other hand, has probably never even heard of the word *plain*. To start with, she's gorgeous — long, silky black hair and big, almond-shaped eyes (she's Japanese-American). Her skin has not one blemish, even with all that junk food. And the way she dresses makes her look even more stunning.

At that meeting, for example, she was wearing these sharply creased, pastel-green, cuffed shorts; a wild Hawaiian shirt tied at her waist, with vibrant colors that perfectly picked up the green; and sandals with crisscrossing ankle straps to her knees. Her hair was swept to one side and held in place with a long, fake-flowered barrette that looked like a Hawaiian lei.

And, as usual, she was scrounging around under her mattress for some new treat. "Let's see, they're in here somewhere," she said, pulling out a Nancy Drew book and throwing it aside. By the way, those books are her other addiction. She has to hide them *and* the junk food because her parents don't approve of either. (They're very strict, and it doesn't help that Claud's sister, Janine, is a real live genius who does *everything* right.)

"Here they are!" Claudia cried out, pulling a bag of malted milk balls from under her pillow. "Who wants some?"

Claudia is our vice-president, mostly because it's her room and her phone. She doesn't really have official duties, like, say Mary Anne.

Mary Anne is our secretary. She keeps the record book, which has a list of all clients' addresses and phone numbers, plus a detailed appointment calendar. As soon as a client calls, Mary Anne checks to see who is available. That means she has to keep track of all the sitting jobs *and* all of our schedules — my ballet classes, Claudia's art classes, Mallory's orthodontist appointments, any family trips . . . it's enough to make your head spin. But for Mary Anne, it's easy. She's incredibly organized. I think she picks that up from her dad, who is a neatness freak. (No one knows what Mary Anne's mom was like, because she died when Mary Anne was little.)

Maybe her mom was caring and shy and sensitive. That's the way Mary Anne is. She cries at *anything* — sad movies, deaths of famous people . . . Dawn says she once almost cried when she saw an abandoned Christmas tree in someone's garbage last January. *That* is sensitive!

Guess who is best friends with Mary Anne

the Shy one? Kristy the Loud Mouth (don't tell Kristy I said that). They even look alike. Mary Anne is petite and has brown hair and brown eyes. She's not a tomboy, though, and she dresses with a kind of neat, preppy style. She used to look much different — little-girl clothes and pigtails, right up through seventh grade. That's because Mr. Spier took a long time to realize Mary Anne had a mind of her own. Thank goodness he remarried. That really loosened him up, and Mary Anne was "allowed" to grow up. In fact, she's the only one of us who has a steady boyfriend. His name is Logan Bruno and Mary Anne thinks he looks *exactly* like her favorite movie star, Cam Geary.

Oh, I didn't say *who* Mary Anne's dad remarried: Dawn Schafer's mom! That's another romantic story. Mr. Spier and Mrs. Schafer both grew up in Stoneybrook. They used to date, but they ended up marrying other people. The Schafers lived in California for years, but then Dawn's parents divorced. Mrs. Schafer moved back to Stoneybrook with Dawn and her younger brother Jeff (Jeff's not here anymore; he decided to move *back* to California with his dad). They moved into this big, old farmhouse that was built in the 1700s. (Know what? It was once a stop on the Underground Railroad, which was an escape route to the North for African-American slaves.) Then Mrs. Schafer and Mr. Spier met again, realized they still loved each other, and got married! Mary Anne and her dad moved into Dawn's house — and *they* lived happily ever after.

Dawn has this long, blonde (almost white) hair, blue eyes, and freckles. She's a real individual, and does what she wants to do. Like eating only health foods — vegetables, fruits, tofu, whole grains, sprouts. She never even gets tempted to eat Claudia's candy. I mean it. Instead, she'll eat whole wheat, unsalted sesame crackers or some other gross thing. To tell you the truth, she has the perfect diet for a ballerina, but I could never stick to it. I mean, I watch my weight, but give me a juicy hamburger over a tofu salad anytime.

Dawn is our alternate officer, which means she takes over whenever anyone else is absent. For a while Stacey McGill moved to New York City, and Dawn took over Stacey's job as treasurer. So the club was minus one member, but calls were pouring in. So guess who got to join? Mallory and I! (We weren't in the original group.) Then Stacey ended up returning to Stoneybrook, and Dawn gave her back her job (gladly), but Mal and I remained members.

Stacey is originally from New York City, by the way, and she knows her way around there like the back of her hand. (Isn't that a weird saying? Do people *really* know the backs of their hands?) Now her dad lives there, while her mom lives in Stoneybrook (they're divorced). I think NYC is the coolest place in the world. Once, when Stacey went there to visit her dad, a bunch of us went along. I saw some incredible dancers there — including a guy I like, named Quint. If I do decide to become a pro, *that's* where I'm going to live.

Like Dawn, Stacey has long, blonde hair. Like Claudia, she really knows how to dress. But Stace is definitely her own person — sophisticated, smart, outgoing, funny, and pretty wild about boys. She's also a diabetic, which means her body can't control the level of sugar in her blood. What does that mean? All I know is that she can't eat sugar, and she has to give herself injections of something called insulin. Can you imagine? I'd probably pass out if I had to do that.

One other thing about Stace. She's a math genius. That's how she became treasurer. I think that's the worst job. Every Monday she has to collect dues from us. (Actually, *paying* the dues is the worst part.) She puts the money in our treasury. Then she pays Charlie Thomas for driving Kristy, and Claudia for part of her phone bill. And she figures out if we have any more expenses, like replacing

Kid-Kit things when they get used up. If anything is left over, we sometimes use it for a
pizza party or some other fun thing.

I mentioned before that there are two associate BSC members. One of them is Logan
Bruno (yes, Mary Anne's boyfriend), and the
other is Shannon Kilbourne. But there's another regular member of the BSC, and I saved
her for last.

She's Mallory Pike, my best friend. Mal is
really sweet and smart, and she loves kids. (If
she *didn't* love kids, she'd be in trouble, because she has seven younger brothers and sisters!) On the outside, we're very different.
She's white and she has red hair, glasses, and
braces. Otherwise, we have *a lot* in common.
We're both junior officers of the BSC, since
we're two years younger than the other members. (That means we get to do everything
except late-night sitting jobs.) We're both the
oldest in our families, but even so, sometimes
our parents treat us like babies. For instance,
Mama and Daddy wouldn't dream of letting
me dress in wild clothes like Claudia does, or
double-pierce my ears like Dawn. They let me
pierce my ears (single), but I practically had
to beg for years. Same with Mal and her parents, only it's worse. Her parents won't let her
get contacts, and she hates wearing glasses.

Let's see, what else . . . oh, we both love

reading, especially horse stories. And we're both good at something creative. With me it's dancing, with Mal it's writing and drawing. You should read her stories. I think they're better than some real books. I know she's going to be a famous children's book author and illustrator someday.

Back to the meeting. We were stuffing ourselves with malt balls (except for Dawn and Stacey, who were eating rice cakes). The phone wasn't ringing, so all you could hear was crunching.

And the scratching of Claudia's charcoal pencil. She was drawing this wild design with five circles in the middle. The circles were arranged just like the Olympics symbol.

"What's that?" I asked.

"I'm trying to come up with a logo for the SMS Sports Festival," Claudia replied. "Mrs. Rosenaur asked me to do it." (Mrs. Rosenaur is one of the gym teachers.)

SMS, by the way, stands for Stoneybrook Middle School (our school). The Sports Festival is an annual event that includes mostly track and swimming. There had been an announcement about it at school that day.

"Ew," Mary Anne mumbled.

"Thanks a lot," Claudia said, putting her hands on her hips.

Mary Anne actually blushed. "Oh, I didn't

24

mean the design," Mary Anne said with a giggle. "I meant Mrs. Rosenaur. I *hate* gym."

"But you're going to sign up for the festival, aren't you?" Dawn said.

"No way," Mary Anne replied. "That's even worse than gym class. It's a competition, and I'm terrible at sports."

"Yeah, but the festival is just for fun," Kristy said. "I mean, there are prizes, but I think the idea is just to participate and have a good time."

Claudia looked up from her pad. "*I* might enter an event, if it's not too embarrassing."

"Well, I'm definitely going to enter one of the track events," Kristy said. "I'm not sure which yet."

"I'm going to do something different," Dawn said. "Like shot put or pole vault or something."

Stacey nodded. "I'm going to enter one of the swimming events."

"Sounds like fun," I said, thinking about the Community Center and my upcoming summer at the pool. "Maybe I'll enter a swimming event, too."

Mal just kind of sat there, looking glum. Sports have never been her strong point. I could see the festival was about the last thing in the world she wanted to talk about.

"Ooooh!" Kristy suddenly blurted out. "I

forgot to tell you guys what happened after lunch today!"

"What?" we asked.

Kristy was practically jumping out of her seat. "After the announcement, Alan Gray and his friends were talking about the Sports Festival. Then Alan started to act jerky, as usual — and then he just, like, *announced* that he could beat me in a race anytime!"

(I should explain that Alan Gray is the most immature guy in the whole school. He's in eighth grade but acts like his brain has been on hold since second grade. He also, unfortunately, has a crush on Kristy.)

"So what did you do?" Stacey asked.

Kristy smiled proudly. "I took up the challenge — and you guys are going to be there!"

"All *right!*" Dawn said.

That was when the phone rang for the first time.

"Hello, Baby-sitters Club," Claudia said.

The "club" part of the meeting had officially ended, and the "baby-sitter" part had begun.

CHAPTER 3

Isn't it funny how when you start thinking about something completely new, all of a sudden it comes up everywhere?

Take swimming, for instance. I'd never really thought much about it before. I mean, I knew *how* to swim, more or less. Daddy and Mama had taught me the breast stroke and the dog paddle at the Jersey shore when I was about eight. But that was it.

Then I had my brainstorm about buying a pool, and suddenly swimming started to take over my life. My family was joining the Community Center, I was thinking of taking lessons, and I was getting all psyched about swimming events in the SMS Sports Festival.

And then there was gym class.

It was Thursday, and the hot weather hadn't let up a bit. Mal and I were sitting on the gymnasium bleachers, chatting. Mal's sort of like Mary Anne, not into gym at all. It's not that she's a *bad* athlete. She just feels very self-conscious. I think she's most comfortable when she's at a desk with a pad and pencils.

Anyway, there we were, when Ms. Walden bounced out of her office with her clipboard and called out, "Okay, who's not here?"

"I'm not!" Maya Condos answered. That was about the hundredth time someone had made that joke this year, but we laughed anyway.

Ms. Walden chuckled and took attendance. Then she looked up and said, "Well, I have a surprise for you girls. Today is your last regular gym class."

We all shrieked so loudly, the sound echoed off the ceiling.

"I hope everyone has a bathing suit that fits," Ms. Walden went on, "because starting next week, the community pool complex will be open during school days, and I'll be taking you there for swim lessons during gym period."

The cheers and groans that followed were about even. As for me, I was thrilled. Free lessons? Great! Maybe by the time the summer started, I'd be able to sign up for intermediate classes on my family membership.

Mal didn't feel the same way. I found that out later, as we were walking back to the gym after forty-five minutes of calisthenics and field hockey. We were both out of breath and *dripping* with glow. Mal wiped her forehead and said, "Well, there's one good thing about going to the pool for gym class."

"What?" I asked.

Mal looked over her shoulder, in the direction of the community pool complex, then thought for a moment. "It's about a five-minute walk there and a five-minute walk back," she said. "So that's ten minutes less gym!"

I laughed. "Mal, you're so *negative*! This'll be great. We'll get out of school for a whole period, and we'll learn how to do something fun."

"I already know how to swim pretty well," Mal said.

"Maybe they'll have more advanced lessons," I suggested. "Or maybe you'll be able to get some coaching for the Sports Festival." Then I remembered how unexcited Mal had been about the Sports Festival at our BSC meeting. "I mean, if you decide to be in it . . ."

"Everybody else is going to be in it, right?" Mal said. "In the BSC, I mean."

"Except Mary Anne," I reminded her.

"You're going to be in it."

"Yeah . . ."

"Well," Mal said with a shrug, "then I will, too."

"Great," I said. I'd never seen Mal so touchy, but I didn't say anything. I couldn't blame her. The weather was enough to put anyone in a bad mood.

It cooled off a little over the weekend, and by Tuesday the sky was clear, and the air was breezy and dry. Tuesday was the day of our first gym class at the community pool complex.

I guess they call it a "complex" because it has three pools — an Olympic-sized swimming pool, a wading pool, and a diving pool (all outdoors). Ms. Walden told us we were going to use the big pool, and I couldn't wait.

"I am *soooo* excited," I exclaimed to Mal as we walked toward the girls' locker room with our class, clutching our swimsuits.

Mal was frowning. And not listening to me. "What's that?" she asked.

"What's what?"

"That noise! Are the *boys* here?"

I looked where she was looking. Sure enough, a door on the other side of a long snack bar said BOYS' SHOWERS. The unmistakable yelling of boys came from inside. "I guess we're sharing the pool with their gym class," I said.

"Oh, *no!*" Mal cried, as if she had to kiss Alan Gray or something. "No one told us that!"

"I know. But what's the big deal?"

"What's the big deal? I only brought the ugliest, babiest bathing suit in the world!"

She held it out, and I have to admit she wasn't lying. It was an out-of-style, faded, one-piece suit with a ruffled skirt. "Oooops . . ." I said, trying not to smile.

"It's not funny," Mal said. "I'm going to look ridiculous. This is so unfair!"

I tried to cheer Mal up, but she sulked while we changed into our suits. Finally I agreed to stand between her and the boys, to block her from view. That made her feel a little better.

So we walked out to the pool, in our suits, Mallory using me as a shield. Her shoulders were hunched, her knees were bent, and she was looking over my shoulder at the boys. "This is *so* embarrassing!" she said.

The boys were all on one side of the pool, and the girls stuck together on the other side. We looked like enemies gathering for war council. The boys were pretending not to notice us, but I could see one or two curious faces staring at Mal and me.

"Uh, Mal," I said. "You know, I have a feeling you're attracting *more* attention by doing this."

"I don't want anyone to see me!" she whispered sharply.

Ms. Walden's voice boomed out from behind us. "Okay, girls, stand in a line by the pool!"

We did. Now we were all facing the boys. By then some of them were whispering to each other and laughing. Mal was dying. Benny Ott, a true goon, was doing a really dumb imitation of a girl's walk, swinging his hips from side to side and making some of his dorky friends laugh.

"Ott, get over here!" the boys' teacher yelled.

"They are so immature!" Mal whispered.

"I know," I agreed.

"I'm *freezing*!" Mal said. "Look!" She held out her arms, which were covered with goose bumps.

"Yeah, it's pretty cool out," I agreed.

"We shouldn't have to get our hair wet! We could catch pneumonia and die!"

"Mal, I don't think it's *that* — "

Ms. Walden's voice interrupted our conversation. "Now, I know you must be at different levels of swimming," she said. "And I'm aware some of you may not swim at all. But don't worry. Today I'm going to give you each a swimming test, and then divide the class into groups. I want you to feel comfortable. Let's go alphabetically . . ."

Mal just stood there, stone-faced. I felt awful for her.

Ms. Walden began testing us, one by one. When Mal's turn finally came, she dived quietly into the water and did a pretty good backstroke, breast stroke, crawl, and dog paddle.

"That was great!" I said as Mal climbed out of the pool.

"Thanks."

Ah-ha! A smile! I actually saw one. I guess Mal was loosening up a little.

"Jessi?" Ms. Walden said. "Come on, your turn."

Suddenly I realized I'd been so concerned with Mal I hadn't thought of myself. I wasn't such a great swimmer. How foolish was *I* going to look?

I dived in and did whatever Ms. Walden asked me to do, which was all the strokes Mal did. I did them my way, slowly and carefully. At one point I saw Ms. Walden whispering with another woman, who looked at me and nodded.

Oh, great, I thought. They're trying to figure out if there's going to be a group slow enough for me.

But when my test was over, Ms. Walden took me aside and said, "Jessi, could you see me after class?"

"Sure," I said.

Remedial swimming. Those were the first words that popped into my head. Ms. Walden — or maybe that other woman — was going to tutor me personally.

Now it was *my* turn to feel awful. I plopped down on the edge of the pool next to Mal. Neither of us said a word.

Finally, when class was over, I approached Ms. Walden. The other woman was standing next to her. She was thin, with short, darkish-blond hair and a wide smile. I tried to smile back.

"Jessi, this is Ms. Cox," Ms. Walden said.

Ms. Cox held out her hand and I shook it. "I was watching you swim before. Have you had dance training?" she asked me.

That wasn't the question I had expected. "Uh-huh," I said. "I take ballet lessons."

Ms. Cox smiled even wider. "I thought so. I could tell by your form in the water — very lyrical and smooth."

"Thanks." Now I *really* couldn't tell what she was getting at.

"Jessi, I wondered if you had ever thought of synchronized swimming," she said, looking much more serious.

I drew a blank. "Uh . . ."

"You don't know what it is," Ms. Cox said with a laugh. "That's all right. Most girls don't at first. You see, I run a program in synchronized swimming here at the pool complex. Basically it's a team of girls, all ages, and we perform routines in the water — sort of like dance routines. I'm always looking for strong swimmers, but most importantly, I need girls with good form. I could use someone with your ballet background."

I looked from Ms. Walden to Ms. Cox. I felt an incredible rush of relief. "Um, well, it sounds like fun," I said. "When are the practices?"

"Fourth period," Ms. Cox replied. "The one right before this."

"Oh, that's my lunch period," I said, disappointed.

"It's all right," Ms. Walden said. "You could take your lunch fifth period, instead of regular gym. That would be easy for me to arrange with the administration — *if* you want to do it."

Swimming *with* dancing — and no gym class? It sounded too good to be true. How could I say no?

"Sure!" I said to Ms. Cox. "I'd love to try it."

"Wonderful!" Ms. Cox replied. "Our next practice is Thursday, right here. See you then!"

CHAPTER 4

Well, Thursday came.

I felt more excited than nervous. But still, when I showed up at the pool complex during fourth period, my stomach was rumbling.

It was a little embarrassing, I have to admit — and I couldn't figure out why it was happening. After all, I'm used to performing in front of crowds.

Then I realized my poor stomach was being faked out. Usually fourth period meant lunch — no wonder it was complaining.

I saw Ms. Cox running toward me (maybe she heard the rumbling). "Jessi, hi!" she called. She had a huge grin, and seemed full of energy.

"Hi," I said.

Ms. Cox turned around and said in a loud voice, "Girls! We have someone new in the class — Jessica Ramsey. Jessi, this is Abby, Monica, Hannah . . ."

She mentioned fifteen names altogether, and after she was done I didn't remember a single one. I guess I *was* nervous.

"Hi," I said again and again. I was really showing off my vocabulary, huh?

"Oh, this is wonderful," Ms. Cox went on. "We finally have an even number in the class. You see, Jessi, we do a lot of work in pairs. With only fifteen girls, that means someone is always switching around. Right, Elise?"

A pretty, raven-haired girl smiled and said, "Yup."

"Elise Coates has been partners with just about everyone in the class," Ms. Cox went on. "But not any more. I'm going to make you two a permanent pair, okay? I think you'll work well together. Take a few minutes, get to know each other, and then Elise can catch you up on some basics." She turned to Elise and said, "Go over the side stroke and the crawl, and show her the standard scull, the tub position, and maybe the tub turn and the back tuck somersault if you have time. I'll be around to help you out."

Huh?

Tub turn? Back tuck somersault? What had I gotten myself into? This was nothing like my first ballet class, where all we did was first- and second-position *pliés* for an hour.

Ms. Cox must have noticed how I was feeling, because she gave me a confident wink and said, "It's not as hard as it sounds." Then she shouted, "Come on, girls. Let's do some warm-ups!"

Elise smiled. Her dark brown eyes warm and friendly. "It's really nice to meet you. Have you ever done any synchro?"

"Uh . . . what?"

"I guess you haven't," Elise said with a laugh. "Synchro is short for synchronized swimming."

"Oh." Boy, did I feel stupid.

"Don't worry," Elise said. "I only started a couple of weeks ago. I'm, like, one of the worst in the class — so just think, with my help, you can be, too!"

I laughed. Thank goodness Elise was so nice. She put me right at ease.

"I have an idea," she said. "This will start to give you a feeling for synchro. Can you do a side stroke and a crawl?"

"Yes!" It felt so good to know *something*.

"Good. Let's do two laps of side stroke and two laps of crawl together. Try to stroke at exactly the same time I do."

"Okay."

Elise stood at the edge of the pool. I stood next to her. "Ready?" she asked.

"Ready."

She jumped in, feet first. So did I.

We swam our four laps, and I was able to match strokes with her pretty well. The trouble was, she was a stronger swimmer and kept getting way ahead of me.

"That was good," Elise said as we climbed out of the pool. "Your presentation is fantastic!"

"Presentation?"

"That's Ms. Cox's word for style. She's always trying to get us to move gracefully. Her big saying is, 'Work hard, but make it look easy.' That's my weak point — but you do it naturally."

"Thanks," I replied. "I guess that's because of my ballet classes. I wish I could swim as fast as you, though."

"Oh, sorry," Elise said with a guilty grin. "I shouldn't have gone so fast. It's just that I'm on the SMS swim team and I'm used to racing."

"You're on the *swim team*?" I said. "But you said you were one of the worst — "

"Synchro's much different than racing. I have strength, but no style."

"And I have style but no strength," I said with a sigh.

"See? It's perfect! That's probably why Ms. Cox put us together. We can coach each other."

I could tell Elise and I were going to get

along — and I was right. The rest of the hour was fun. *Exhausting*, but fun. First Elise showed me how to "scull." That's the way you support your body in the water. While you're lying on your back, you sort of sweep your arms away from your body and then back in, keeping your fingers together. To move headfirst, you keep your wrists "hyperextended" (bent upward). To move feetfirst, you keep your wrists "flexed" (bent downward). It's actually a little more complicated than that, but that's the basic idea.

Anyway, we practiced sculling for a long time, until I got the hang of it. Then Elise taught me the "tub" position, in which you lie on your back and draw your knees up close to your chin. It's like a sitting position, only you're facing upward. Sound easy? It's not, because you have to scull at the same time, to keep your body near the surface.

We never got to the somersault, but it didn't matter. I was hooked on synchro — and I had a new friend.

Ms. Cox could tell, too. She came over to us three times during the hour. At the end, she said, "Jessi, you look fabulous. You're going to be ready for competition in no time."

I started to say "competition?" but the word stuck in my throat. I mean, synchro was fun, but I was just *beginning*. I learned ballet movement fast, too, but I didn't have my first recital until after a year of classes!

Before I could say anything to Elise, Ms. Cox was making an announcement to the class: "Girls, I have some good news! I just got word from the school. It's official — we're going to be a part of the SMS Sports Festival!"

"Yea!" screamed Elise (and all the other girls).

"We're going to do a demonstration in two eight-member groups," Ms. Cox continued, "and then pairs will compete with each other for medals."

There was another burst of happy screaming, and everyone started talking excitedly. "Isn't that great, Jessi?" Elise said to me.

It *was* great. I honestly did feel excited. I also felt like I was in over my head. "I guess," I answered.

Elise looked concerned. "What?"

"Nothing. It's just that, well, I'm so far behind everybody."

"Oh, Jessi, you are such a perfectionist!" Elise said with a laugh. "The way *you* learn, you're going to have no problem being ready. I can tell."

"You think so?" I said.

"*Think* so? I *know* so! Jessi, this'll be so much fun!"

You know what? I believed Elise. Her energy was so positive. And to tell you the truth, deep down inside I feel pretty confident when it comes to anything physical. (I get that confidence from ballet lessons — dance is similar to sports in many ways.)

I knew it would be a lot of work for me — and for Elise, too. But there was something else I knew. I knew we could do it.

When I returned home after school that day, I couldn't wait to tell everyone the news. The first person I saw was Becca, curled up in front of the TV. A car commercial was just ending.

"Becca, guess what?" I cried.

"Ssshhh!" Becca said. "Watch this with me, Jessi! It's the Olympic trials."

I sat down and watched some incredibly fast women running a hundred-meter sprint.

"Wow!" Becca exclaimed. "They look so muscle-y!"

"Fast, too," I said.

"I wish we could *go* to the Olympics! That would be fun."

After the race, the announcer started blabbing some boring statistics, so I said, "Guess what, Becca?"

"What?"

"I'm going to be in the SMS Sports Festival!"

Becca's eyes lit up. "Really?"

I told her about the class and Elise and Ms.

Cox. She listened with a big smile and said, "I'm going to sit in front during the show and say, 'Yea, Jessi!' "

"You better!"

"And then," Becca went on breathlessly, "when *I'm* in sixth grade, you have to come and cheer for me, because I'm going to be in the festival, too!" She paused. Then added, "Maybe." (Becca is sort of shy.)

"All *riiight!*" I said. We gave each other high-fives, low-fives, and as many different kinds of fives as we could think of.

Another race was starting, so we sat back and watched. Becca was staring so hard her mouth was hanging open. I almost laughed.

We watched and watched until another commercial came on. Then Becca sat up straight and said, "Jessi? They have the Olympics in a different place each time, right?"

"Uh-huh."

"Are they ever going to have them in Stoneybrook?"

"I doubt it."

"Not even if, like, the mayor calls up way, way in advance, and says they can use the new high school track?"

I smiled. "No, Becca. They always have the Olympics in bigger places then Stoneybrook."

Becca slumped back in the couch. She looked crushed, as if I'd just told her there was no Santa Claus. "That stinks. I wish they would have them right here."

"Yeah, I know what you mean," I said sympathetically.

I began walking toward the kitchen. But I kept thinking of what Becca had said.

The Olympics. In Stoneybrook.

Maybe it wasn't such a far-fetched idea.

Maybe there was something I could do about it.

The idea rolled around in my head all night. Actually it was more than just an idea. It was a project, the kind of thing Kristy would think up. I wasn't sure it would work, but I was *dying* to bring it up at a BSC meeting.

Luckily I didn't have long to die, because the next day was Friday. I arrived at the meeting early, figuring I'd talk it over with Kristy the Idea Genius first.

But I couldn't. Not while she was belly-down on Claudia's carpet.

That's right. Belly-down, fanning her arms and legs inward and outward — and Stacey was doing the same right next to her.

"Let your hands *meet* in front of your face," Kristy was saying, "then push against the water. See? Push . . . Push . . ."

I nearly cracked up. The two of them were doing the breast stroke on the floor. Claudia was sitting on her bed, eating an Oreo cookie.

When she saw me, she smiled and shrugged. "Welcome to BSC swimming camp," she said.

Stacey sat up. "Oh, hi, Jessi!" she exclaimed, her face turning bright red.

Kristy glanced over her shoulder. She looked sort of like a turtle.

Claudia burst into giggles, smacking her hand over her mouth to stop the Oreo crumbs from spraying out.

Stacey started giggling, too. Finally I gave in.

Kristy sat up and brushed herself off. "Well . . . hrrmph," she said, clearing her throat (I could tell she was fighting back a smile). "I guess it's almost time to start."

"What were you doing?" I asked.

"Stacey wants to do the breast stroke in the Sports Festival, so I was coaching her," Kristy said.

"Kristy's much faster than I am," Stacey added. "We practiced a little in gym class."

"But Stacey has great form," Kristy said.

That sounded familiar.

"Hey, I was enjoying the show," Claudia chimed in. "Keep going."

"Oh?" Kristy said with a mock-angry voice. "And what event are *you* going to enter? Speed eating?"

Claudia pulled another Oreo out of the bag

and examined it. "Oh, something track-orientated, I think."

"*Track-orientated?*" Kristy repeated.

We howled with laughter.

That was when Mary Anne and Dawn entered the room. "What's so funny?" Mary Anne asked.

"Kristy and Stacey were swimming on the rug," Claudia said.

"Claudia was being strange," Kristy said.

Mary Anne and Dawn gave each other a they've-just-gone-nuts look.

Then Kristy looked at the clock, which said 5:29. Quickly she put on her visor and sat on her chair. I could hear footsteps running down the hall. Mallory appeared in the doorway, looking guilty. "Am I — ?" she began.

"Order!" Kristy barked.

Mal slipped in, relieved she wasn't late.

"Any new business?" asked Kristy.

Shrugs and head shakes around the room.

I was getting ready to tell everyone about my new idea, when Mal asked, "How did your synchronized swimming class go?"

"Fine," I said. "We're going to be in the SMS Sports Festival."

"Really? You must catch on fast, Jessi."

"I don't know about that," I replied. "I have a long way to go."

"That's okay," Stacey said. "You saw how bad my breast stroke was, right? That's going to be my event. I don't care if I come in last. I just want to have a good time."

"Me, too," said Dawn. "That's why I'm going to enter the javelin throw."

"*Javelin throw?*" Claudia remarked, as she pulled a bag of potato chips from a drawer in her night table. "Are you serious?"

"Do you really know how to do that?" Mary Anne asked.

"I'm learning," Dawn said. "I think it's perfect. No one else knows how to do it, so how bad could I be?"

"Hmm . . . makes sense," Stacey said, chomping on a potato chip. "Maybe you could try something like that, Mary Anne."

"Yeah, like the shot put," Dawn suggested. "No one's entered that yet."

"Yeah, right," Mary Anne said with a laugh. "You have to be a moose just to lift one of those things."

"You could work out," Claudia said mischievously.

"Forget it," Mary Anne replied. "You guys can tell me all about it the next day."

"What about you, Kristy?" Claudia asked. "You haven't told us what you're going to do."

A big smile spread across Kristy's face. "I

thought you'd never ask. I think I'll tackle the obstacle course — "

"Ugh," Claudia said. "That sounds hard."

"It *is* hard," Kristy said, "but I think it'll be even harder for Alan Gray."

"Ooh, Kristy, you *didn't*!" Stacey said.

"Well, not yet," Kristy replied. "I'm going to bet him a week of 'personal service' that my time is faster than his, which means whoever loses has to do what the winner wants for a whole week."

"Whoa, great!" Stacey said, clapping her hands.

"What if he says no?" Claudia asked.

"I have to challenge him the right way," Kristy said. "In public, like in the cafeteria, where a lot of people can hear. Then he'll be too embarrassed to refuse."

"Oooh, I want to be there!" Stacey said.

"Me, too!" cried Dawn.

"He asked for it," Claudia added.

Rrrrrring!

We stopped chattering. Claudia picked up the phone and said, "Hello, Baby-sitters Club . . ." She paused for a moment. "What? . . . A million dollars? . . . Me? . . . Are you sure? . . ."

We all sat forward.

"But I don't have a checking account. . . . What? You'll deliver it in cash? To my house?

Um, no thanks, I wouldn't know where to put it. 'Bye!"

As she started to put the receiver down, Stacey screamed. "Are you crazy? Don't hang — "

Click went the receiver.

You could practically feel everyone's jaw drop to the floor.

Claudia calmly reached under her mattress and felt around for some other junk food. "Money isn't everything, you know," she said casually.

"Claudia . . ." Kristy said, "Was that . . . did you . . . who . . ."

Suddenly Claudia cracked up. "It was a *recording*!" she said. "Some voice trying to sell carpet cleaning, that's all. Fooled you!"

We heaved a sigh. But before anyone could say a word, the phone rang again.

This time it was a client. We managed to calm down and assign the job. After Claudia hung up, the room became quiet — a perfect time for me to say what I'd been waiting to say.

"Guys, I have a great idea," was how I began. "Yesterday I was watching the Olympic trials with Becca, and she was so excited about them, and I told her about the SMS Sports Festival, and she said she wished the Olympics were in Stoneybrook. Well, she looked really sad, and at first I couldn't figure out why. Then I realized she was seeing all this exciting stuff on TV, then hearing about *my* event — and what was there for her? Nothing. So I thought, maybe we could organize something for the kids. You know, a Mini-Olympics or something."

Finally, I said it. Half of me expected everyone to groan, and half expected everyone to love it.

The second half was right.

"What a *fantastic* idea," Dawn said.

"We could invite all our charges," Mary Anne said. "It could be a way of thanking our clients for the jobs they give us."

Kristy nodded. From the look in her eye, I could tell the idea sponge was working. "We could have a three-legged race, a potato-sack race, a basketball-shooting contest . . ."

"Maybe some silly events, too," Claudia suggested. "Like a race where everyone has to make a funny face, or a grapefruit throwing contest."

"Ew," Mallory said.

"We could have an award for each kid," Dawn said, "so no one will feel left out."

Everyone starting throwing in suggestions, and you know what? That was all we talked about for the rest of the meeting (except for when we took two or three more phone calls).

By the time the meeting was over, I felt fantastic. It looked like the Mini-Olympics was going to happen — and it was my idea!

CHAPTER 6

Monday

Wow, was I in for a surprise on Saturday. I thought it was going to be an easy job. Daytime baby-sitting at my own house usually is. I just open the door and let the kids run around like crazy. I hardly have to do anything.

Not this time. I simply mentioned your idea, Jessi. I never dreamed how my brothers and sisters would react...

Let me explain something. When Kristy writes "I hardly have to do anything," it's not really true. She always gets involved with her kids — playing softball, hide-and-seek, tag, you name it. She's a great sitter, especially with her own brothers and sisters.

So when Kristy says she had a rough time, you *know* it was rough.

The day started out perfectly — clear and sunny. Kristy's mom and stepdad had gone furniture shopping and her older brothers were out with friends. So Kristy was spending a few hours with David Michael and Karen (they're both seven), Andrew (four), and Emily Michelle (almost three).

She did just what she wrote — let them loose in the yard. And you should see the Brewers' yard. Picture a football field with a mansion stuck in the middle of it. Well, maybe I'm exaggerating, but not by much. Anyway, in the back is a great climbing tree and a playground set, and in the garage are tons of outdoor games.

Practically the whole neighborhood was outside, and soon a bunch of kids came over to play. So Kristy was watching not only her own four charges, but Linny and Hannie Papadakis, Bill and Melody Korman, and Scott and Timmy Hsu.

Ten kids — with just Kristy to baby-sit!

Well, Kristy was delighted. (Don't forget, she's the one who organized an actual softball team.)

Then came the Big Mistake.

"Hey, guys," she called out. "Come over here. I have a surprise for you." (An old baby-sitting trick — if you want kids to come running, tell them you have a surprise.)

They each yelled some version of: "Surprise? What? What is it?" And, of course, they came running.

"Have you guys been watching the Olympics?" asked Kristy.

There was a chorus of "Yeahs" and "yeses" and "uh-huhs."

"Well," Kristy continued, "my friend Jessi had an idea at the last Baby-sitters Club meeting. How would you guys like to have a Mini-Olympics of your own — just for kids?"

"YEEEEAAAAAAHHH!"

The response nearly burst Kristy's eardrums.

"Okay, okay!" she said. "Now, we have some ideas for events, but why don't you tell me what you'd like to do?"

"Horse-racing!" Melody shouted.

"It has to be simple," Kristy said. "You know, like three-legged races."

"Yeah! Three-legged races!" David Michael said.

"A basketball-shooting contest!" Timmy said.

"I once went to a picnic where they had potato-sack races," Hannie said.

"Roller-skating races!" Melody said.

"Long jump!" Scott yelled.

"Volley ball!" Karen said.

"Magic show!" Linny shouted.

"There are no *magic shows* in the Olympics!" Hannie said, rolling her eyes.

"Weight lifting!" Bill suggested.

"Whoa, whoa!" Kristy said. "I can't remember all of these. Let me go inside and get a pen and paper. Meanwhile, if you guys want to be in shape, you better start training!"

Kristy ran inside, and by the time she came back out, the backyard was in chaos.

David Michael and Linny were both trying to do chin-ups on tree branches. Timmy was doing push-ups. Melody was doing jumping jacks. Hannie and Karen were setting up croquet wickets. Scott and Bill were racing each other around the yard. Andrew was dragging one of Watson's old dumbbells out of the garage.

Kristy had to laugh. They were taking their Olympics so seriously.

"What's this?" Kristy asked Hannie and Karen. "Olympic croquet?"

"No, it's an obstacle course," Hannie replied. "We're going to run around these — left, right, left, right — then jump over the plastic bench, then climb the tree to the second branch, then come down, then run to the driveway and jump over it."

"Wow," Kristy said. "Hey, did you guys know that I'm going to run an obstacle course, too?"

Hannie's eyes lit up. "Maybe you can practice with us!"

"Sure!"

Oh, did I mention what happened when Kristy challenged Alan Gray? Well, it worked exactly the way she thought it would. She did it in the cafeteria and his friends started to tease him. Then he got red in the face and accepted.

But that wasn't all. Alan started bragging to his friends in gym class, his teacher heard him — and guess what? Alan's teacher got together with Kristy's teacher, and they decided it would be fun to have a special series of "spectator events" — one-on-one races to be held throughout the festival. And Alan and Kristy were the first two people they asked.

Well, Alan wasn't crazy about the idea, but

he had to say yes when Kristy agreed. So they officially became the first two participants in "The Great SMS Coed Obstacle Challenge"! I was almost as excited about *that* as I was about my own event.

Back to Kristy's backyard. The kids were having a blast. Kristy raced with them, coached them in basketball shooting, set up a volleyball net, showed them how to roller skate, set up a refreshment table with juices and water, broke up fights. . . .

Whew. I'm glad I wasn't sitting that day. I wouldn't have survived in one piece.

At first Kristy didn't mind it. She was having a lot of fun. But after an hour or so, she began wishing someone would come home to help her out.

And that was when Andrew started sobbing.

Kristy turned around and saw him lying on the grass. She ran to him, thinking he'd hurt himself badly. "Andrew, what happened?" she asked. "Are you okay?"

"Ahhh caaaa dooo aaaaathing!" he whined.

Kristy lifted him off the ground and put his head on her shoulder. "All right . . ." she said in a soothing voice. "Now, can you tell me what happened, slowly?"

"I — I — I — can't do — do — anything!"

Andrew said, hiccuping his words between sobs.

"What do you mean?" Kristy asked.

"I — I can't do any push-ups, I'm slower than — than everybody, my legs aren't long enough to jump over things." He choked back a couple of sniffles. "Everybody's better than me!"

Part of Kristy *wanted* to say, "That's all? That's what you got me so scared about?" but us baby-sitters know better than that (well, most of the time). She gave him a big hug and said, "You really feel sad, huh?"

"Yeah . . ." Andrew replied in a teeny voice.

"Would you like me to coach you?"

Andrew's lips curled into a little smile. "Okay."

"Good. We'll figure out something you're good at. What do you want to start with?"

Andrew sat up and pointed to the basketball hoop. "That!"

Kristy ran to the driveway with him and picked up the ball. "This might be too hard," she said. "But give it a try."

Andrew lifted the ball to his shoulders and heaved it, but it didn't go anywhere near the basket.

Kristy grabbed the ball as it came down. "Try it underhanded, like this." She demonstrated an underhand shot that went right in. "You might get more power that way."

Andrew tried, but the ball went crashing into the garage door.

"Uh . . . let's do something else," Kristy said quickly. "I don't think any four-year-olds are ready for a net this high. It's . . . regulation height, you know. The same height that pro basketball players use."

"Oh," Andrew said.

Next Andrew wanted to try some weight lifting, but he wasn't even strong enough to lift Watson's lightest dumbbell. "*I* can do it," Linny bragged. He yanked *two* of them off the ground and held them over his head.

You can guess what Kristy wanted to call *him* (I'll give you a hint: Linny was holding one in each hand). Instead she said, "Linny, that's not fair. You're eight years old!"

"Yup," said Linny proudly.

"Come on, Andrew," Kristy said, "let's try Karen and Hannie's obstacle course."

Well, Andrew had fun running around the first few wickets, but his foot got caught in the last one and he fell to the ground.

Next he tried a three-legged race with Karen. Karen tried to be gentle, but Andrew didn't have a knack for it at all. He couldn't take even two steps without falling.

Roller skates, volleyball, long jumping —

Kristy tried everything she could think of. But Andrew just kept feeling worse and worse. Even if he could do something, the other kids could do it better.

By the time her parents came home, Andrew was in his room, sucking his thumb and crying. Bill and Linny were racing around, accusing each other of cheating. Timmy and David Michael were fighting over where one of them had landed in a long jump. Melody was holding an ice pack on her ankle.

And Kristy? Well, she felt as if she needed to be scraped off the floor.

Maybe my great idea wasn't so great after all.

CHAPTER 7

*B*oom . . . *Boom . . . Boom . . . Boom . . .*

That was the beat of a dance tune blasting over the pool loudspeakers. What tune was it? I can't remember. The only thing I was paying attention to was the beat — and Ms. Cox's voice:

"Extend right leg, extend left leg, layout, oyster. . . . good!"

Boom . . . Boom . . . Boom . . . Boom . . .

"Tub position, right side scissors kick, left arm crawl, left side scissors kick, right arm crawl!"

The entire class swam back and forth in rhythm, following Ms. Cox's instructions. Sometimes we bumped into each other, but we mostly stayed in even lines.

Synchronized swimming, as you've probably noticed, is always performed to music. In fact, some fancy pools have underwater speakers. But in the not-so-fancy Stoneybrook community pool complex, we use a big tape player on the deck. The music has to be unbelievably loud for us to hear anything underwater. And Ms. Cox had to use a bullhorn to be heard over it.

Let me tell you something else about synchro. It *looks* easy, but it's not. Not only are you performing a choreographed dance routine, but you have to worry about staying afloat *and* keeping a constant distance from everyone else. You can't stop moving, and sometimes you're doing one stroke per beat.

"Finish waterwheel . . . good, Hannah! . . . layout . . . back tuck somersault . . . head up . . . arms . . . that's the end!"

Ms. Cox pressed the button on the tape recorder, and the music stopped in the middle of the tune. You could hear the frantic breathing of sixteen exhausted girls.

"Good work!" came Ms. Cox's voice. "Abby, that back tuck was great. Kate, you're like a new person today! All of you, congratulations. Let's take a breather."

As we climbed out of the pool, Ms. Cox approached Elise and me. "You girls okay?"

"Sure," Elise said.

"Are you feeling tired, Jessi?" Ms. Cox said. "You were a little behind."

"No, I'm okay," I replied.

"Good," said Ms. Cox. "Elise, your presentation is much better, but keep your strokes smaller, closer to your body. All right?"

"Sure," Elise said. "Thanks."

As Ms. Cox walked away, Elise and I looked at each other and sighed. For awhile, neither of us said anything.

It was Elise who finally broke the silence. "That felt awful."

I nodded. "I know. All I could think about was keeping up with everybody. I mean, I've learned all the strokes, but I have to *think* so much that my form is starting to stink."

"*Your* form? I still feel like a water buffalo in there. I must have bumped into twenty people."

"Which is hard to do in a class of sixteen."

We both cracked a smile, but we were too depressed to laugh. Here it was, four weeks after I'd started synchro, and Elise and I were both lagging behind the rest of the class. Ms. Cox was complimenting everyone except us.

It was so weird. I had never felt awkward or slow when I began taking ballet class. At least I don't remember feeling that way.

"Okay, girls," Ms. Cox called out. "We've got about ten more minutes. When you're feeling rested, you can do some work in pairs."

I looked at Elise. "Want to?"

"Yeah, but let's talk about the routine for a minute, okay? I'm confused about what happens after the back tuck somersault."

Oh, that's another thing. Since I'm the one with the dance training, Ms. Cox had asked me to choreograph our pairs routines. What's a "pairs routine"? It's the only part of the competition we create ourselves. Each pair gets to do one, but only after performing a required series of figures. So I jumped at the chance to choreograph — and of course, I made up something much too complicated. It looked great, with these weird ancient Egyptian-style hand and head movements. The only problem was, both Elise and I were having trouble *doing* it.

After we discussed the routine we jumped in and got to work. We tried to go through the whole routine, but after only four measures or so we were completely out of whack.

"Oops, sorry," Elise said, treading water.

"No, my fault. I was slowing us down."

"Hey, Jessi, help me with my arms a minute. Is this right?"

Treading furiously with her legs, Elise began moving her hands and head above the water. Have you ever seen those old Egyptian paintings on the sides of vases? You know, like Queen Nefertiti and King Tut, with heads turned to the side and their arms and hands bent in angular positions? Well, that's what I was trying to do in the routine.

I hate to say it, but Elise looked terrible.

To do the routine right, you have to form sharp angles and graceful movements. Elise was all jerky, almost as if she were making fun of the moves.

"That's basically it," I said, "but try not to work so hard at it. It should be more like this . . ."

Then I tried to demonstrate it — and promptly began to sink. My arms were great, by my head was underwater!

"Pkaccchh!" I said (more or less), as I stopped being Nefertiti and started frantically treading water. "Why can't I keep myself afloat?"

"You really have to push off with your legs," Elise explained. "Watch."

We worked like that for a while, until Ms. Cox blew her whistle signalling the end of class. Then we hauled ourselves out of the pool and walked to the lockers.

The locker room was noisy with laughter and conversation and gossip, but Elise and I hardly said a word as we changed into our street clothes.

It wasn't until we were walking back to school that I said, "I can't believe the festival is coming up so soon."

Elise sighed. "Yeah. Do you think we'll be ready?"

"I hope so," I replied. I didn't dare say *no*, but that was how I was feeling.

"I'm sort of nervous about this," Elise admitted.

"Me, too."

"You know, it's funny. Yesterday the swim team had a meet, and I won a first place in the butterfly — "

"You didn't tell me that!" I said. "That's great!"

Elise smiled modestly. "Well, I wasn't saying it to brag or anything. What I meant was, it's weird how one thing comes easily to me and the other one doesn't."

"I know what you mean!" I said. "I feel the same way. Yesterday in ballet class I did this incredible combination that ended with a triple *pirouette* and an *entrechat*."

"A what and a what?" Elise said.

"Those are two really hard movements I never used to be able to do."

"I thought they were French pastries," Elise said.

I couldn't help but laugh, and boy, did it feel good. "I don't know, Elise. I guess I'm taking this too seriously, but it's hard not to. I mean, one day my ballet teacher is telling me I should train to be professional, and the next day I come here and feel like a total dork."

Elise looked at me and frowned. "You're not

thinking of dropping out, are you?"

"No way!" I stopped in my tracks. "Are you?"

"No way, *José*! I want to keep working till I get it right!"

"Me, too." Then an idea came to me. "Why don't we get together and practice by ourselves?"

Elise's eyes lit up. "Yeah! The pool's open for the season now, so we can use it after school and on weekends."

"Every spare minute," I said. "Like . . . after school today?"

"Sure!" Elise said. "If my parents will let me."

I looked at my watch. "Well, we have three minutes before next period starts. Last one to the pay phone is a rotten egg!"

We ran the rest of the way to the school. I was beginning to feel inspired. I kept thinking of the Olympic athletes I saw on TV. *They* worked day and night to get where they wanted to be.

If that was what it took for them, that's what it would take for us.

CHAPTER 8

Friday

It's funny what the Mini-Olympics is bringing out in kids. It's as if all their personality traits become exaggerated. If they're competitive to begin with, they become terrors — and if they're non-athletic to begin with, they act like turtles and pull in their heads.

Oh well, thus speaks the famous Dr. Stacey McGill, child psychologist. I just wish I had made that brilliant observation before I sat for Charlotte Johanssen last night. It would have helped a lot...

I think Stacey was too hard on herself. She always means well. Anyway, no one's perfect.

Let me tell you about Charlotte. She's eight years old, but she's in fourth grade already, because her parents let her skip. She is *very* smart (so are her parents — her mom's a doctor and her dad's an engineer), but she's also fun and sensitive and friendly. In fact, she was the first kid in the neighborhood who didn't avoid us because we were black. Other kids were acting like we were poisonous or something, but not Char. She made friends with Becca right away. That meant a lot to our family.

Char's really cute, with chestnut brown hair, dark eyes, and a great dimply smile — and she's an only child, which makes sitting jobs especially easy. Her favorite sitter is Stacey. They call each other "almost sisters."

The evening Stacey sat for Char was warm and muggy. Stacey ran straight to the Johanssens' house from the community pool complex (she was using it after school to work on her breast stroke). By the time she got there, she felt all sticky and gross.

Putting on her best smile, she rang the doorbell. "Hi! Anybody home?" she called through the front screen door.

Dr. Johanssen came into the living room,

holding a briefcase. "Hi, Stace!" she said, pulling the door open. "Thanks for coming. My meeting shouldn't last more than two hours, but at any rate, Mr. Johanssen will be home around dinnertime. I left the emergency numbers by the phone."

"Okay," Stacey said.

"Char's in her room, reading," Dr. Johanssen went on, hurrying out the door. "Help yourself to anything in the fridge. 'Bye!"

" 'Bye!"

Stacey shut the door behind her and walked upstairs. She knocked on Charlotte's door. "Can I come in?"

"Stacey?" said Char's voice. "Hi! I didn't hear you downstairs."

Stacey pushed the door open. Char was sitting on her bed, holding a set of earphones. A pile of books was on her left and a cassette recorder on her right. "Hi! What're you doing?" Stacey asked.

"Listening to 'Peter and the Wolf.' It's exactly the same words as this." She held up an open copy of the book. "I can read it, but I love hearing the music, too. Want to hear?" She pulled the earphone plug out of the machine.

"Sure," Stacey said.

They listened for awhile, until Charlotte looked at her Mickey Mouse clock on the wall and announced it was time to walk Carrot.

Carrot is Charlotte's pet schnauzer. He was snoozing in the shade under the maple tree in the Johanssens' backyard, but he sprang up the moment he heard the back door open.

Charlotte took a leash off a hook near the door and called out, "Want to go bye-bye?"

Carrot went wild, running around in circles and yapping excitedly.

Giggling, Charlotte raced after him and clipped the leash on his collar. Then she and Stacey started walking with him down the driveway.

"Did you come from school?" Char asked Stacey.

"Yup," Stacey answered.

"Then how come your hair's all wet?"

"I was practicing at the community pool. I'm going to be doing the breast stroke in the SMS Sports Festival."

"You *are*?" Charlotte seemed amazed.

Stacey laughed. "Yeah. Why does that surprise you?"

"I don't know."

That was when Stacey thought about my idea. "Hey, Char. Have you heard about the Mini-Olympics?"

"Uh-huh," Charlotte said, stopping while Carrot sniffed a tree.

"Do you want to be in it?"

Charlotte made a sour face. "Yuck."

"Come on, Char. Why not?"

"I *hate* all that stuff," Charlotte said. "I hate sports and I hate gym class. Besides, all these people are going to be there, and you *know* I get nervous in front of an audience."

Stacey did know. A long time ago, Charlotte was supposed to recite a passage from the book *Charlie and the Chocolate Factory* in a kids' pageant, and she got so frightened she forgot the whole thing.

Stacey knew she shouldn't push Charlotte. But when she thought about how much fun the kids were going to have in their Olympics she wanted so badly for Charlotte to be included.

"I guarantee it won't be this big, high-pressure thing," Stacey said. "There'll be silly races, awards, refreshments, all kinds of fun stuff. And your friends are going to be in it. Really, Char, I *know* you'll have a good time."

Charlotte just stared silently at the road as Carrot pulled her forward.

"What if Becca said she'd be in it?" Stacey suggested.

Charlotte shrugged. "I don't know . . ."

"Hey, why don't we invite her over? Would you like that?"

Finally Charlotte perked up. "Sure!"

They finished walking Carrot around the

block. Then, when they returned to the Johanssens', Stacey called our house.

Guess who answered the phone. Becca. When Stacey asked her over, she got all excited. In minutes Becca was at Charlotte's. Stacey took the two girls into the backyard. She wanted to try out some ideas. "Char," Stacey said, "do you still have bubble stuff in your bathroom?"

"Yeah."

"Can you get it? Two bottles would be better, if you have them."

"Sure."

"I'll go too!" Becca cried.

The girls raced inside. Sure enough, they each returned with a bottle of bubble soap and two wands.

"Okay," Stacey said. "We're going to have a bubble contest!"

"Yippee!" Charlotte yelled.

Well, the two of them had the *best* time. Becca and Charlotte spent the next ten minutes blowing big, wobbly bubbles and running after them.

The next game Stacey played with them was "Trash Fashion Models." You wear the tops of plastic garbage cans like hats (*clean* ones — you wash them off first), then you try to walk in a straight line without letting them fall — like those runway models you see on TV. That was good for a few more minutes of giggles and squeals.

Next they ran inside for a snack. Stacey prepared bowls of fresh fruit with crackers. As they were eating, she noticed something strange on the floor — a big, light brown balloon in the shape of a hand. "What is *that*?" she asked Charlotte.

"Oh, one of Mom's surgical gloves," Char said. "She has boxes of them. Sometimes she lets me blow them up like balloons."

Stacey picked it up and tapped it into the air. "How about this game? Keep it up — whoever lets it fall loses!"

"*Yeeaaaah!*" Charlotte and Becca squealed. They ran outside, batting the glove upward. Stacey said it was the weirdest sight, seeing these two girls hitting a *hand* in the air.

By the time they finished *that*, it was starting to get dark. The three of them collapsed onto the grass with happy sighs.

"That was fun, wasn't it?" Stacey said.

"Yeah," the girls agreed.

"You know, the events in the Mini-Olympics are going to be just like these," Stacey said. "So do you think you guys want to be in it?"

She said it innocently, and I think she expected the girls to say yes enthusiastically. But both of them became kind of quiet.

75

"I don't know," Becca replied. "Maybe." (It turns out that Becca was more interested in the *idea* of the Olympics than in actually being in them — but how was Stacey to know?)

Charlotte just shrugged and looked glum.

Before Stacey could say anything, Becca jumped up. "Uh-oh. I forgot, I promised Mamma I'd help set the table for dinner."

Charlotte and Stacey followed her down the driveway. Becca waved. " 'Bye! See you at school tomorrow!"

" 'Bye!" Char yelled back.

Char turned to go inside without even looking at Stacey. It was as if she were completely shut off inside.

"Char?" Stacey said, following her into the house. "Is everything okay?"

"Uh-huh," Charlotte said.

"Um, are you mad at me for something?"

Charlotte shook her head. "No . . . you're mad at *me*."

"I am?"

"Yeah," Charlotte said. "Aren't you?"

"Well . . . why *would* I be?"

"Because I don't want to be in the Mini-Olympics."

Stacey felt about two inches high. She realized she *had* been pushing Charlotte too hard. She hadn't meant to, but Charlotte felt awful. "Oh, Char . . . I'm sorry. I don't mean to force you into something you don't like. Really. I —I just open my mouth too much. You don't have to be in the Mini-Olympics. I'll like you just as much either way."

"You will?" Charlotte said.

"Of course."

"Are we still 'almost sisters'?"

Stacey smiled a big smile. "You'd better believe it."

They both felt better. And Stacey vowed never to bring up the Mini-Olympics in front of Char again.

CHAPTER 9

"They said yes!" Dawn screamed, as she and Mary Anne ran into Claudia's room.

"Yeaaaaa!"

You should have heard the noise. I could swear the windows rattled. Why? Because we had solved the biggest problem facing the Mini-Olympics: where to have it. We had talked about using Dawn and Mary Anne's big backyard, but we had to wait till they asked permission.

"Both Richard and my mom think it's a great idea," Dawn went on. "All we have to do is give them a date — any Friday after school or any Saturday during the day."

"That's perfect," Kristy said. "What about the Saturday after the SMS Sports Festival?"

"Perfect," Stacey said.

"Sounds good to me," I added.

"I move we do it then," Kristy said.

"I'll write it down," Mary Anne said, picking up the club record book.

"All in favor . . . ?" Kristy said.

"*Must* we, Kristy?" Claudia moaned.

"All in favor . . . ?" Kristy repeated.

"Aye," we said wearily.

"All opposed?"

No one answered.

"Motion carried. The official date of the Mini-Olympics will be the Saturday immediately following the Sports Festival."

" 'Immediately following'?" Claudia said with a sly smile. "What's wrong with 'after'?"

Kristy shot her a Look, but Claudia just handed her an open bag of pretzels and said, "Sorry! Peace offering!"

Kristy grinned and grabbed a handful. "Offer accepted."

Mary Anne was scribbling in the record book. "So that's two weeks from this Saturday, right?"

"Wood," Kristy said. She meant to say "Right," but her mouth was full of pretzel.

Over a month had passed since I had suggested the Mini-Olympics — and the idea had caught on like wildfire! At least thirty kids had already signed up, and most of their parents had agreed to help supervise.

Pretty amazing, huh? Just call me Jessi, Idea Sponge II.

Riinnnng!

Claudia picked up the receiver. "Hello, Baby-sitters Club. . . . Oh, hi, Mrs. Hobart! . . . Yes. . . . Oh! Sure they can. . . . Uh-huh. . . . Uh-huh. . . . Two weeks from Saturday. . . . You're welcome. 'Bye!"

"Two weeks from Saturday?" Mary Anne said. "But we *can't* do a job that day — "

Claudia shook her head. "That wasn't about a job," she said. "Mrs. Hobart wanted to ask us if her boys could be in the Mini-Olympics."

"All of them?" I asked.

"The three younger ones. James wants to be in the three-legged race, Mathew wants to be in a regular race, and Johnny wants to do weight lifting."

"But he's only four!" Stacey commented.

"Well, Archie Rodowsky and Jamie Newton want to lift weights, too," Mary Anne said. "I think all the four-year-olds have been talking about that for some reason."

"We could get some kind of plastic weight set," Kristy suggested.

Mary Anne removed a folded sheet of paper from the record book. "I think we need to update our schedule of events . . . let's see, three-legged — James Hobart . . ."

"Oh!" Dawn said. "I sat for the Braddock kids last night. Haley decided to enter the funny-face race, and Matthew wants to be in the Wiffle ball derby."

See what I mean? There were new entrants every day. I have to admit it was a boost to my ego. And I really needed one, considering how I was feeling about my synchro class.

"You know," Kristy said, "I think we should just let the kids enter as many things as they want. It'll be easier that way."

"You're right," Mary Anne replied, putting down her pencil.

"Hey, Stace, did you talk to Charlotte?" Kristy asked. (No one had read the notebook entry yet.)

Stacey nodded. "She's not going to be in it."

Kristy seemed shocked. "No? Why not?"

"She just doesn't like sports," Stacey said with a shrug. "Or crowds."

"What?" Kristy said. "Maybe we should talk to her again."

"I don't know about that, Kristy," Mary Anne said.

"She feels pretty awful," Stacey added.

"Yeah!" said Mallory. "So *what* if she doesn't want to be in the Mini-Olympics? Not everyone does, you know."

Wow. I'd never heard Mal stand up to Kristy like that. Us junior members usually keep a pretty low profile.

Something was still bugging Mal. For the last few weeks she hadn't been herself. I wished I didn't feel so distant from her, but between ballet class and after-school synchro, we just weren't seeing much of each other.

I promised myself that I'd talk to her as soon as I could.

Kristy was pretty cool about Mal's reaction. "Yeah, you're right. I guess I get carried away."

"We can't *all* be big stars like you and Alan Gray," Stacey said mischievously, breaking the tense mood.

"I hear *The New York Times* is going to cover your event at the Sports Festival," Claudia added.

"What?" Kristy said. "You don't — not the — " Then her face turned red. "Hey, no fair, guys! Now you're ganging up on me!"

"It *is* news all over school, Kristy," Dawn said. "People are making a bigger deal out of it than the Summer Olympics."

"Uh, let's change the subject." (Kristy looked embarrassed, but I could tell she kind of liked the attention.) "How's your swimming class going, Jessi?"

"Oh, fine," I answered. "I like it."

"I'm amazed you can learn all that new stuff so fast," Mary Anne said. "You are *so* talented!"

"Someday she'll be deciding between the *real* Olympics and the New York City Ballet," Stacey added.

This is what I wanted to say: "Are you kidding? I'm the worst in the class!" But I couldn't bring myself to do it. Why? I'm not sure. Maybe I didn't think they would believe me. Maybe I didn't want to let them down, since they all seemed to think I was some kind of super-athlete. Maybe I didn't want to jinx myself.

Whatever it was, this is what I *did* say: "It's fun. You should try it sometime."

A few of my friends nodded, but Mary Anne said, "Thanks but no thanks. I'd probably drown."

"Boy, you really do love sports, don't you?" Stacey said with a laugh. "You ought to get together with Charlotte."

Stacey meant that jokingly, but it made me stop and think. Becca had told me about the afternoon at the Johanssens', and I could imagine how awkward Char felt. Suddenly I realized a way to make her feel better. "You know, that's not a bad idea," I said.

"What's not?" Stacey asked.

"Well, maybe you should call Charlotte, Mary Anne. Tell her *you're* not going to be in the Sports Festival. She looks up to you. Maybe when she hears that, she won't feel so bad about not being in the Mini-Olympics."

"That's a *great* idea!" Stacey agreed.

"Sure," Mary Anne said. "I'd love to do that."

The phone rang again, and the meeting returned to normal. We had solved a lot of problems. The Mini-Olympics was becoming a reality. Charlotte would soon be feeling better, I was sure. Mal — well, I'd have to figure out what was wrong with her.

But for some reason, my mind kept going back to the pool. All I could think about was the placement of my hands in a tub turn. It was going to be a long two weeks.

CHAPTER 10

mondy

I cant beleive their are still twelv more days til the mini - Olimpicts Olimpyks. If I have to go thru one more job like Saterday at the Pike's, I think I'll dorp dead. And I was the lucky one. At laest I ended up with two legs intacked. Pour malery. mal was the BSC's first causalty. cashul accident case of the training seasin.

You make it sound so terrible, Claud. It's not that bad.

may be not now, but you should have seen the extpretion on your face when it happened, mal...

As you can see, Claudia and Mal had Pike Duty that Saturday. What's Pike Duty? It's sitting for the seven younger Pike brothers and sisters.

They are good kids, but they are a handful. Besides Mal, these are their names, in order of . . . appearance (I guess you could call it that): Adam, Byron, and Jordan (ten-year-old triplets); Vanessa (nine); Nicholas (eight); Margo (seven); and Claire (five). I could also count Frodo, but he's a hamster.

When Claudia reached Mal's house, she found the whole Pike clan in the backyard. The kids were running around like crazy, dragging a weight-lifting set onto the driveway, setting up markers for a race, piling up potato sacks and old rags, arranging an ice bucket and refreshments on a card table. And screaming and yelling. It made Kristy's sitting experience sound positively peaceful.

"Hi, guys!" Claudia called out as she strolled into the backyard.

"Hi, Claud!" Mal called back.

"Hi!" yelled Vanessa and a few of the others.

"Yo," said Jordan Pike, who was walking around with his chest out and his shoulders lifted high. As he turned away, he sort of waddled from leg to leg. "Come on, look lively!" he yelled, clapping his hands. "Let's go!"

Claudia giggled. "What got into *him*?" she asked.

"He's Spuds Diamond today," Mal said.

"Who?"

"Spuds Diamond. He's the coach of some Olympic thing. Jordan saw him yesterday on TV and wants to be just like him."

"Does Spuds Diamond have something wrong with his shoulders?"

Mal laughed. "No. Jordan thinks he looks muscular when he scrunches them up like that."

"Oh," Claudia said, smiling.

"Okay, let's start the training program!" Jordan bellowed, trying to use a deep voice. "Adam, Byron, you guys look a little soft in the belly — "

"Look who's talking!" Adam said.

"Fatso!" Byron remarked.

Jordan sucked in his stomach (which must have been hard to do, because actually he's pretty skinny). "You guys run a few sprints between the markers. Nicky, let's see a few push-ups. Vanessa, you and Margo do sit-ups — "

"We want to lift weights!" Vanessa protested.

"Well, okay . . . Claire, you can do jumping jacks."

"Silly jumps!" Claire squealed. "Like this." She began jumping up and down, making weird faces, her arms and legs flailing all over the place.

Jordan swaggered over to the card table. He opened up a container of brown powder, spooned some into a glass, then poured in water from a pitcher.

"What is *that*?" Claudia asked. It looked absolutely disgusting.

Jordan raised his eyebrows as if Claud had just asked the world's dumbest question. "Brewer's yeast," he said confidently. "It's very rare in nature," Jordan said as he began mixing the drink. It became muddier and grosser looking, and Jordan's face quickly lost its macho grin.

"It's my dad's," Mal whispered to Claud. "He tried it once and couldn't stand it."

"And he let Jordan take some?" Claudia said.

"Dad *warned* him, but Jordan said — "

"*Yuuullllk . . . . ucccchhh!*"

Spuds Diamond suddenly disappeared. He was replaced by Jordan Pike.

"Yuchh! . . . yuchh! . . . yuchh! . . ." he kept repeating, his face contorted. "I have to go to the hospital!"

Mal rushed to the table and grabbed a pitcher of orange juice. Pouring some into a cup, she said "Here, have this. It'll wash away the taste."

Jordan swallowed it down like a thirsty person in the desert. When he came up for air, he was still gagging, but not as much.

"Oooo," he said with a shiver, "don't *ever* drink that. I'm going to throw it away."

"Good idea," Mal said.

Then . . . back came Spuds Diamond. Up went the shoulders, down went the voice. "Okay, time for aerobics! Line up!"

"Jor*dannnn*!" Vanessa complained. She and Margo were lifting weights with Marilyn and Carolyn Arnold, who had just come over.

"Call me Coach!" Jordan corrected her. "Now, come on! Let's start with . . . um, running in place."

"Wait here," Mal said to Claudia. "I'll be back."

The kids had only been running for a few seconds when Mal returned with a cassette recorder. She set it on the table and played a dance-pop song with a strong beat.

This brought the kids to life. After a while Jordan switched them to jumping jacks, then push-ups, then squat thrusts (basically, he stopped whenever *he* couldn't do any more).

Well, the music acted like a magnet. Soon

89

the yard was filled with kids from around the neighborhood. Buddy and Suzi Barrett showed up, then Haley and Matt Braddock, then Jenny Prezzioso, then the Kuhn kids.

Pretty soon Jordan's aerobics class was out of control. The kids split off and started practicing for their events. Their noise became almost unbearable. It was more like a Screamers' Olympics. Even Matt Braddock, who is deaf, was signing like crazy and making loud noises to emphasize what he was trying to say.

At this point, the sitting job was actually pretty easy for Claud and Mal. Mal was just watching, and even though Claudia felt like having fun with the kids, she didn't want to leave Mal alone.

So the two of them sat. And sat. And sat. Mal wasn't very talkative.

"Mal?" Claudia finally said. "Is everything okay?"

"Mm-hm."

"The kids look like they're having fun. Want to join them?"

"Not right now," Mal said.

So they sat some more. In front of them, Jordan and Buddy were climbing into potato sacks. "We'll start here and end up at the tree stump, okay?" Jordan said, pointing to an old brown stump that's almost invisible in a corner of the yard.

"Okay," Buddy replied.

"Ready, set, go!" Jordan called out.

The boys were off and hopping. And then, according to Claudia, Mal began to fidget a little. After a moment, she stood up and said, "I want to try a race!"

Claudia was surprised. "Which one?" she asked.

"Potato-sack!" Mal·grabbed two more sacks from the pile and gave one to Claud. They stepped into them at Jordan's starting line, just as he and Buddy were coming back.

"Watch out for the stump," Buddy warned.

"I know," Mal said, "I live here, remember?"

"Okay, ready?" Claudia asked.

"Yup," Mal answered.

"Set . . . go!"

They began hopping. Buddy and Jordan cheered them on. Surprisingly, Mal was whooping and yelling and really moving fast. In fact, she reached the stump way before Claudia did.

And that was when she collapsed to the ground.

"Yeeooooow!" Mal wailed, grabbing her left ankle.

Claudia jumped out of her sack. Jordan and Buddy ran to them. "We *told* you to watch out for the stump!" Jordan exclaimed.

"Easy, Jordan," Claudia said. "Mal's hurt." She knelt down and put her arm around Mal's shoulder. "Are you okay?"

Mal was grimacing. "I — I think I twisted my ankle," she replied.

"Let's see," Claud said.

Mal took her hand away. The ankle wasn't swollen, so Claudia asked, "Can you move it?"

Mal tried. "It hurts a little."

"A little?" Claud asked. "Can you stand on it? Here, let me help you." She moved her arm under Mal's shoulders for support and lifted.

Mal stood up on her right foot. But when she tried to shift to her left, her knee buckled. "Owww!"

Fortunately Claud was still holding on. "Uh-oh," she said. "I think you better go to the doctor when your parents get home. Come on. You should sit down."

Claudia helped Mal to a beach chair by the refreshment table. Most of the kids, who had been watching the episode, began going back to their "training."

Mal sat down, keeping her ankle up. By that time, they could see some swelling.

"Looks like you sprained it, all right," Claudia said.

"Darn," Mal replied. "Oh, well. I guess

there's no way I can be in the Sports Festival now."

"Oh, it's okay," Claudia said. "There'll be another one next year. Let me go inside and get an ice pack."

But Mal's reaction struck Claudia as kind of strange. She didn't seem at all upset about missing the Festival. Claud thought she actually sounded glad.

That night, after Claudia told me what had happened, I called Mal. "How are you?" I asked her. "I heard about your ankle. Did you go to the doctor?"

"Yeah," Mal said. "It's a sprain. I have to keep off it for a couple of weeks. I have to use crutches."

"That's awful," I said.

"I'm really upset. I mean, what with the Sports Festival and all. Oh, well. At least it'll be okay by the time school ends."

Now, Mal may be a great writer, but she is *not* a great actress. At least not over the phone. I could tell she wasn't terribly upset about missing the Festival. So why was she making believe? I felt that she didn't trust me or something.

Or maybe I was just tired. We wrapped up our conversation, and I went right to bed.

CHAPTER 11

"Let's . . . try it . . . again! Okay?"

"Wait . . . wait . . . phew . . . okay, ready."

The first voice was mine and the second voice was Elise's. Can you guess what we were doing? You got it — practicing.

For at least the two hundredth time.

It was already Tuesday, D-day minus one. Just one day before the SMS Sports Festival! I had re-choreographed part of our pairs routine, trying to make it easier. We had practiced every day after school (except ballet class days) *and* on weekends for two whole weeks. How did we feel about it? How was our confidence after all that?

Don't ask.

We were still having trouble with the routine — but we were determined to get it right.

"One, two, ready, go," I said. "Head, head, arm, arm, out, in, left, right . . ."

That was where I always stopped speaking.

It's hard to talk, swim, and dance at the same time.

Elise was doing the moves right, more or less. She definitely *was* more graceful, but still rough around the edges. I wished I could bring Mme Noelle to one of these practices. *She* could help Elise.

As for me, well, I still tended to sink into the water below my mouth a lot, but I was getting stronger.

We came to the end of the routine. We hadn't been perfect, but it was the best we'd ever done.

"Want to rest a minute?" I asked.

"Let's do the group exercise," Elise suggested. "At least we can get *those* strokes down."

We worked through that routine, which consisted of the basic moves we'd learned in the class. By now we knew them in our sleep.

Finally we took a rest. Together we hopped onto the side of the pool and caught our breaths. At the other end, a few kids and a grownup were swimming lazy laps, back and forth.

I looked at them longingly. "They seem so relaxed," I said.

Elise sighed. "Well, *they* don't have a competition tomorrow.

"Yeah."

We sat silently for a few minutes. My mind was fried. Even though the pool was quiet, I kept hearing the dance music Ms. Cox always used in class. My body seemed to be rocking back and forth as if I were still in the water. I've always been a hard worker, but I didn't think I'd ever worked *this* hard.

And yet, I wasn't sure how well we were going to stack up against the others. I wished we could have practiced with another pair, just to compare.

"Elise," I said, "have you noticed that we never see any of the other pairs working out here after hours?"

"I guess they don't *need* to. Unlike us."

"It's too bad," I said. "If we could just see them, it would be such a help. We could tell right away if we're doing things right."

"Yeah." Elise nodded, then began dangling her feet in the water. Her brow was squinched up, as if she were deep in thought.

"Jessi?" she finally said.

"Uh-huh?"

"We haven't talked much about tomorrow — I mean, *really* talked."

"What do you mean?"

"Well . . . are you as scared of this as I am?"

I hesitated. Then I said, "We're making really good progress, and we're *so* far ahead of where we were when we started, and our moves aren't as awkward . . ." It was no use. I couldn't lie. "Yeah," I said. "I'm scared out of my mind."

"I just *know* we're going to embarrass ourselves!" Elise exclaimed.

"Maybe we should run away."

"Or hire doubles to take our place."

"Or secretly drain the pool!"

We looked at each other and smiled. It was nice to know Elise and I had a similar sense of humor. "This is so weird," I said. "We've been practicing together for — how long? A month and a half? And we don't even really know each other."

Elise laughed. "I *know*! I was thinking the same thing. We'll have to do something together after this is over."

"Yeah!"

Then we turned back toward the pool. There wasn't time for any more conversation, not during our last big practice.

I realized something then. I wasn't sure whether Elise and I would end up being friends or not, but we did have one thing in common: When we put our minds to something, nothing stopped us.

Even if it meant making fools of ourselves.

"One last try?" I asked.

Elise looked at the clock above the pool. "We have time. Let's go for it — make this the best one ever!"

We jumped into the water. This time I didn't shout out instructions. I couldn't see or hear Elise very well, but we'd performed the routine so many times I could *tell* exactly what she was doing. It was like having ESP. And every time I did catch a glimpse of her, we were in perfect synch.

When we finished, we grabbed onto the side of the pool and caught our breaths.

"Well," Elise said. "What did you think?"

I exhaled heavily. "We still don't *look* terrific, but at least we know the strokes are okay."

An unfamiliar voice interrupted our conversation. "You girls look fantastic. Are you on a team or something?"

It was the grownup who had been swimming on the other side of the pool. He was a trim, gray-haired man with a friendly smile.

"Yeah," Elise said. "We have a competition tomorrow."

"Well, good luck," the man said. "Although I don't think you'll need it."

With that, he waved good-bye and headed for the lockers.

"I wish *he* were one of the judges," Elise said.

"He's probably never seen synchro swimming in his life," I replied.

We pulled ourselves up and trudged toward the girls' showers. The *slap-slapping* of our feet echoed in the early evening air.

"Well," Elise said, "look at it this way: By this time tomorrow it will be over."

"Thank goodness," I replied.

In the doorway to the locker room, I looked over my shoulder. The sight of the pool gave me a dull headache. Then I thought: today was the *last day* I'd be using the community pool complex to practice.

What a relief!

Elise and I changed out of our suits. My headache had traveled down to my stomach, which felt fluttery and nauseous. I didn't think I'd be able to eat dinner. I didn't think I'd be able to sleep.

Insomnia and an empty stomach. What a great way to go into a swimming competition.

It was hard to believe that just a few weeks earlier, I had actually asked my parents for a pool. The way I was feeling that evening, if I never saw a pool again in my life, it would be too soon.

CHAPTER 12

I didn't want to move.

The morning sun was streaming through the cracks in my blinds, and my radio alarm had turned on with a weather report. "Another bright, sunny, late spring day," the announcer was saying. "The kind of day that makes you glad to be alive!"

That was what *she* thought.

I turned off the radio and pulled the covers over my head.

It couldn't be time yet. It couldn't be the morning of the festival.

I felt as if I had slept about ten minutes the whole night. I know for sure I'd woken up at least three times. I kept having this horrible dream: The festival had begun, and I was swimming in the group synchro demonstration, but with my eyes closed. When I opened my eyes, I realized the song had ended and the rest of the class had stopped — except for

Elise and me. Elise was doing butterfly laps so fast she was making waves. The others were sitting at the edge of the pool, staring at us and laughing. Ms. Cox was yelling, "You look tired, Jessi! Hurry up!" And worst of all, Mme Noelle was there, scowling and shaking her head. I wanted to stop, but I couldn't. My arms and legs kept moving and moving, but Elise's waves were pushing me under the water. I started to sink . . . and that was when I'd wake up.

Just a few more minutes of sleep. That was all I needed. Maybe that would wash away the memory of the dream. I shut my eyes tight.

I don't know whether I slept or not, but my eyes finally sprang open when I heard a knock at my door.

"Jessi? Are you up?"

It was Mama.

"Uh-huh," I said in a groggy voice, my back to the door.

I must not have sounded too convincing. The door opened and Mama peered in. "Are you all right, baby?" she asked.

"Mm-hm," I mumbled.

She sat at the edge of my bed. "This doesn't sound like the Jessica Ramsey I know. She'd already be eating her second bowl of cereal. You sure you're feeling okay —or is this an imposter in bed?"

I finally turned around and sat up. Mama

was looking at me. She was smiling, but her eyes were full of sympathy and concern.

"Mama . . ." I said, trying to think of the right words. "You know, you and Daddy don't *have* to come to the Sports Festival today."

"Is *that* what's bothering you, sweetheart?" Mama said.

I nodded meekly.

"But you've been working so hard, Jessi. Of course we want to see you."

"But Mama . . ." I felt close to tears, so I took a deep breath and tried to look away. "It's not like ballet. I — I can't get it right . . ."

There it was. A tear started rolling down my cheek. Another one followed it, then another.

Mama snuggled closer and put her arm around me. "You are being so *hard* on yourself. We know you just started this class a few weeks ago. I think it's wonderful you can even *be* in the festival after such a short time."

"Yeah, but wait till you see the other girls. They really know what they're doing."

"Jessi," Mama said, "remember when we first moved here, and you thought all the classes at your new school were so tough? You came home with a seventy-five on a math test and you were heartbroken. You worked so hard and pulled your average up — but it's never been as high as it was in Oakley."

"Yeah, but I'm doing the best I can," I said.

"*You* always said that's what counts the most."

Mama nodded. "I still say it. And I know that's the way you are, Jessi — no matter what you do, you do your *best*. With ballet, with schoolwork, with baby-sitting, and with swimming." She paused and raised her eyebrow at me. "Unless you've been sneaking away to the movies all those evenings after school."

I smiled for the first time. "No."

"Well, then you've done all you can do, Jessi, and that's enough. The results don't matter, it's the effort. And don't you worry about embarrassing us. As long as we know you did your best, we'll be proud of you."

"You mean that?"

Mama laughed and gave me a big hug. "Of course I do! Now come on downstairs and eat your breakfast."

"Okay," I said as she left. "And thanks."

Well, Mama's words did mean a lot to me. At least they got me out of bed. I knew I *had* done my best, and I knew she and Daddy weren't going to be ashamed of me. That was great.

But what about the rest of the school? While my parents sat there, being proud of my "effort," all of SMS would be laughing at Elise and me.

Needless to say, I didn't eat much. I trudged off to school with my stomach in knots. Thank goodness classes had been suspended for the festival. I don't think I could have sat through one without spacing out.

I felt like a big old sack filled with gloominess.

Then something changed. My gloominess started to seep out. Maybe it was the blue sky and the refreshing spring breeze. Maybe it was the yelling and laughing I could hear almost two blocks from the school. Maybe it was the sight of banners and flags and posters all over the school grounds.

As I got closer, I could hear someone trying to blow a fanfare on a bugle or trumpet. It was pathetically out of tune, but voices screamed "Charge!" afterward, then burst out laughing. In a corner of the playing field, several students and grownups were busily hammering and sawing, constructing a concession stand.

It was *exciting*. You couldn't help but feel it. I almost walked onto the field, until I remembered I had agreed to meet Mallory in front of the school.

I only had to wait about five minutes before one of the Pike station wagons came rolling to a stop in front of me. Mr. Pike slid out, ran around to the passenger side, and opened the door. He helped Mallory out, then reached in for her crutches. "Jessi," he said, turning to me with a smile, "I leave her in your capable hands."

"Okay!" I said.

"Great! See you later!"

" 'Bye!" Mal and I called back.

As he drove away, Mal began *slowly* hoisting herself toward the field.

"You're pretty good at that," I said.

"Thanks," Mal replied. "It's actually not as bad as it looks. My doctor says I'll only have to use these for a week or so, just to keep the weight off."

"*Testing . . . testing . . . oh, what a beautiful morrrning . . .*"

"Booo!"

"Stop the singing!"

A few students were razzing one of the teachers who was testing a microphone. Mal and I laughed.

"Everyone's having such a great time," Mal said. "And I had to go and sprain my ankle. Figures, huh?"

I shook my head sympathetically, but I wasn't convinced. Why couldn't Mal just *admit* she didn't want to be in the festival? I almost asked her right then and there, but it didn't seem like the right time.

I had the strangest feeling — if I hadn't known better, I would have thought Mal sprained her ankle on purpose.

We made our way across the field, and I helped Mal take a seat in the front row of the bleachers.

"When's the synchro?" she asked.

"The swimming events are last," I said. "They're at the pool complex and the whole crowd's going to have to get up and walk there."

"You have a long wait," Mal said.

"Yeah," I replied.

If I didn't chicken out first.

By nine o'clock the stands were full of students, parents, and teachers. Stacey was sitting behind Mal and me, waiting for the swimming events, too. Mama, Daddy, Squirt, and Aunt Cecelia were seated toward the back. I could see a few members of my synchro class scattered around.

Kristy, Claudia, and Dawn were on the sidelines. Every once in a while they would do some jumping jacks, but mostly they gabbed with each other.

"Is this working?" boomed the voice of Mr. Taylor, the SMS principal, over the sound system. (He was sitting in a booth at the top of the stands.)

"*Yes!*" screamed about three hundred kids' voices.

"I guess so! Well, thank you all for coming to the Stoneybrook Middle School's Annual Sports Festival!"

"*Yeaaaaa!*" replied even more voices.

"Before we get started, I have a few words to say . . ."

"A few" turned into this long, boring speech. I think he thanked just about everyone in the school.

When he *finally* finished, the cheering was so loud that Squirt started to cry. I could see Mama holding him while Daddy and Aunt Cecelia tried to comfort him.

"The first event . . . the hundred-yard dash!" Mr. Taylor called out.

Starting with the hundred-yard dash was a great idea. It's a very short, very exciting race — and Kristy was in it! (Yes, in addition to the race with Alan.)

"Yeaaaaa, Kristy!" I shrieked.

"On your marks . . . get set . . . *go!*" said Mr. Taylor.

Bang!

I couldn't believe it — there was an actual starting pistol.

"Waaaaaaaah!"

There went Squirt again. At this point I was just hoping he wasn't going to be scarred for life.

You should have seen Kristy go. The sinews in her legs were bulging out. Her jaw was clenched, and her hair was blown straight back from her face. She looked like a pro!

And she came in second out of six —

and first among the girls!

I cheered loudly. I had no idea she was so fast. When she stepped up to receive her silver medal, the other BSCers on the sidelines yelled in unison, "Yea, President!" (to Kristy's embarrassment).

Next were a couple of longer events —two footraces and a relay race. They were exciting, too, but not as exciting as . . . the backward quarter-mile.

Why a *backward* race? Well, I guess it was a way to get as many of the nonjock students involved as possible (all the jocks were in the serious events). Sure enough, the kids who lined up were . . . well, definitely not jocks.

Take Claudia. She was wearing electric-pink track shorts with a turquoise racing stripe, a matching top with cut-off sleeves, brand-new high top track shoes with no socks, and floral-print suspenders! Her hair was pulled up on top of her head and held in place with a silver barrette in the shape of the Olympic symbol. If it had been an athletic-wear fashion show, she would have won.

And if it had been a comedy event, she definitely would have been close. The minute the pistol went off, the contestants started running backward. The oval-shaped track is divided into six lanes, but hardly any of the contestants paid attention. A heavyset guy rammed right into Janet Gates, who shoved him off the track. Justin Forbes turned around too far and tripped over his own two feet. Woody Jefferson tripped over *him*. Alex Kurtzman ran off the track and didn't seem to be able to aim himself back on. Claudia managed to stay on her feet, but she was running strangely — on her tiptoes, so that her hair bounced up and down like a horse's tail.

It was *hilarious*. I don't even remember who won the race.

The javelin throw was one of the next events. And since it was something that nobody normally did (in gym class or on the track team), everyone was pretty much on the same level. Dawn didn't win, but she threw the javelin beautifully, in a perfect arc. She seemed a little disappointed, but I was proud of her.

I thought about Mary Anne then. I understood why she didn't want to participate, but it was too bad she didn't even want to come to the festival. She would have enjoyed it.

That was what I was thinking when I went to the concession stand to get some lemonade for Mal and me —and guess who was behind the counter?

"Mary Anne!" I said. "I didn't know you were here."

"Hi!" Mary Anne answered. "Well, I *wasn't* going to be here. Charlotte talked me into it."

"*Charlotte?*"

Mary Anne laughed. "Can you believe it? Remember when I said I was going to call her? Well, I told her I wasn't going to be in the festival and she shouldn't worry about not being in the Mini-Olympics. I said there was too much emphasis on sports in school, and when were they going to realize that not *everyone* wants to be a jock. And you know what she said? 'You sound angry — like you really want to be in it but you can't.' "

"Were you?" I asked. "Angry, I mean."

Mary Anne shrugged. "I guess so. I mean, here was this big rah-rah event for something not everyone was good at. It was, like, forget about the rest of you klutzes. I said to Char, 'Sure I want to be in it, but I don't want to embarrass myself!' And *she* said, 'Why don't you sell hot dogs or something? Then you can be part of it, anyway. Don't they need people to do that?' "

"Leave it to Charlotte," I said.

Mary Anne smiled. "So what can I get you? Root beer? Lemonade?"

Before I could make a choice, Mr. Taylor's voice boomed out again:

"And now for the event you've been waiting for: our first installment of The Great SMS Coed Obstacle Challenge — pitting Kristy Thomas against Alan Gray!"

110

CHAPTER 13

Mary Anne and I cheered for Kristy. Then I said, "Lemonade! Two!"

"Okay," Mary Anne replied. She grabbed a pitcher and quickly poured two cupfuls, spilling a lot of it on the counter. "Here, take them! Don't miss the race!"

"Thanks!" I paid her, then ran back to my seat.

As I settled myself next to Mallory, she squeezed my hand. "Ooh, this is exciting!" she said.

"I know, I know!" I replied.

The stands grew quiet. I think by that time the whole school knew about the bet. Besides, how much more dramatic can you get? One against one, boy against girl — even kids who didn't know Kristy and Alan were on the edges of their seats.

We watched the set-up crew lay out the obstacles in two identical courses, so Kristy and

Alan could run at the same time. Both courses began on the side of the goalpost and curved around on the grass, following the track. First Kristy and Alan would have to run about fifty yards, then do a long jump over a sandpit (they'd have to do that close together since the pit was pretty narrow), then jump over three low hurdles, then high jump over a pre-set bar, then zigzag around a half-dozen traffic cones, then step through another half-dozen car tires, then sprint the last fifty or so yards to the finish line. It was *tough*.

I felt a shiver run up my spine. There was Kristy, alone under the goalpost, running in place, shaking out her arms and legs, stretching her neck. Then she looked around the stands and started waving to people and giving the thumbs-up sign. I couldn't believe how confident and calm she looked. Me? I was a nervous wreck just watching her.

Alan was on the track, clowning for the crowd. He'd flex his arm (which was pretty puny), then push his bicep up so it looked bigger. Then he'd mimic whatever Kristy was doing, only with exaggerated "feminine" gestures — you know, the way some guys like to imitate girls? No one laughed, but that didn't stop him. *Then* Alan would execute a super-fast set of push-ups, as if to show everyone how athletic he *really* was.

It was disgusting. But that's Alan.

Unfortunately, you could tell he was in good shape. His legs seemed strong, his push-ups were perfect, and in track clothes he just looked like a jock.

"If he wins, I'll die," Stacey said over my shoulder.

"I'll hit him with my crutch," added Mal.

"I just hope this wasn't a dumb idea," Stacey said.

I looked back at her. "Kristy? Have a dumb idea?"

"Well, there's a first time for everything," Stacey said.

"Ladies and gentlemen." Mr. Taylor's voice crackled over the loudspeaker. "These two brave eighth-graders are the first to take the challenge — and in that sense, they're both winners already!"

Stacey leaned over to me and Mal again. "Yeah, but the *real* winner gets to have a personal servant all week!"

"Can you imagine Kristy being a servant?" I asked.

Stacey rolled her eyes. "Not in a million years!"

Kristy was strolling to the starting line, still waving and smiling.

"*On your marks!*" Mr. Taylor boomed.

"What is she doing?" Stacey asked.

"I hope she's not *too* confident!" Mal said. *"Get set!"*

Kristy and Alan crouched by their starting tapes. Alan said something to her, and Kristy just laughed at him.

"Don't get distracted, Kristy!" I said under my breath.

"Go!"

Bang!

Kristy stumbled.

I thought I was going to have a heart attack. Mal and Stacey gasped.

Alan shot forward. His legs pumped away at full speed.

Kristy recovered right away. She'd lost only a split second, but that cost her a lot of ground.

She started running like crazy. She reached the sandpit just as Alan was jumping over it.

Whump! He landed off-balance on his rear end, then fell to his right — and Kristy came flying over the pit!

I closed my eyes. When I opened them, Kristy and Alan were tangled on the ground, frantically pushing each other away.

They scrambled to their feet and took off again. The hurdles were next. Kristy reached hers first. She leaped — and kicked it flat on the ground. Alan cleared his with room to spare.

"Ohhhhhh," I moaned.

Kristy and Alan both sailed over the second hurdle, then the third . . . almost. Alan's sneaker caught the hurdle after he was over it, and *that* one tumbled to the ground.

And then Alan looked over his shoulder to see what had happened. That slowed him down, and Kristy pulled ahead.

"Yaaaayyy!" we yelled.

Next was the high jump. Kristy plunged forward, headfirst. Her shoulders went over, her waist, her knees . . . but her sneakers clipped the bar.

She landed in a heap. The bar wobbled . . . and wobbled . . . and stopped wobbling. It had stayed!

But Kristy spent a second or two watching the bar, and Alan just dove over his, no problem.

Alan pulled ahead. Next came the traffic cones. Kristy and Alan ran around them, taking small, quick steps.

Kristy must have been a little flustered, because she kicked over the first two while Alan ran around his perfectly.

Then he stepped into the open center of the first car tire. Lifting his legs high, he stepped into the second, the third . . .

And his foot got stuck in the fourth. He lost his balance but broke his fall with his hands.

Kristy passed him, taking slow, high steps.

Alan's face turned bright red.

After the tires, it was a sprint to the finish line. Alan picked himself up and ran through the last two tires.

Kristy reached the open field first — but not by much. She dug in with her legs, put her head down, and *ran*.

Alan was about two steps behind her, but he closed that distance right away. He looked furious.

"Yeeaaaaaaaaahhhhh!" We were on our feet, screaming our lungs out. All around us, people were standing and screaming with us.

Kristy and Alan were neck and neck for a few yards. But Alan moved ahead, and you could tell he was picking up speed.

My stomach sank. He was going to win. Mal and Stacey were frozen with shock.

But Kristy must have been saving some energy. All at once, her legs actually seemed to grow longer. She pulled up even with Alan.

And he did a double take! He was so sure he'd win, he couldn't believe Kristy had caught up with him. You could see the shock in his face.

That was all Kristy needed. She kept her eyes forward, sped ahead . . . and they crossed the finish line together!

At least that was what it looked like from

where we were sitting. By the finish line, people were cheering wildly. They could see something we couldn't from our angle.

But what was it?

The festival officials (teachers) were talking seriously with one another, looking at a stopwatch and gesturing toward the finish line. Kristy and Alan were circling around by themselves, huffing and puffing and ignoring each other.

The officials nodded in agreement, then one of them signaled something to Mr. Taylor.

"We have a winner, ladies and gentlemen!" Mr. Taylor announced.

I held my breath. Mal was clutching my hand and Stacey had a grip on my shoulder.

"The winner of the first installment of the Great SMS Coed Obstacle Challenge is . . . Kristy Thomas!"

Well, I yelled so loudly I thought my lungs were going to collapse. Stacey and I hugged each other and jumped up and down. Then we bent over and included Mal in our hug.

As for Kristy — well, she was eating it up. She was leaping around in the end zone, pumping her arms and whooping. Not exactly *modest*, but that's Kristy.

I never thought I'd feel sorry for Alan Gray, but the look on his face was pathetic. He was crushed. His shoulders were slumped and his mouth was puckered as if he'd just bitten into a lemon.

Then, with a grand sweep of her arms, Kristy snapped her fingers at Alan and pointed to a spot right next to her. Alan stared at her, stunned. Then he said something to her. But Kristy shot him a hard look.

He fumed and sputtered, but I guess even he realized a deal was a deal. Red-faced, he stood at Kristy's side.

His week as Kristy's servant had just begun.

The rest of the track and field events seemed to fly by. Before long Mr. Taylor announced that the swimming events would be starting in twenty minutes.

It was Sweating Time for me. And I mean sweating — this was *not* glow and *not* perspiration. Kristy and Alan's race had taken my mind off my own event, but that was over now.

Half of me hoped everyone would just go home. Then I wouldn't have to embarrass myself.

But no such luck. The crowd, including us, filed through the gate and made a left turn toward the pool complex.

"Hey, Jessi!" I heard Elise's voice call.

I turned around and saw her running toward me. "There you are!" she said. "I didn't see you in the stands!"

Boy, did I feel relieved. I introduced Elise to Mal and Stacey. Soon Mary Anne and Dawn caught up to us, then Claudia did — and finally Kristy did, with Alan tagging behind.

Congratulations and hugs were flying around. People in the crowd seemed to swarm around Kristy especially. Everyone (except Alan) seemed so carefree — laughing and joking and talking a mile a minute.

I felt ill.

Stacey ran ahead of us, because the regular swimming events were going to take place first. When Elise and I arrived at the pool complex, we went straight to the locker room to change.

I'm afraid to say I didn't even see Stacey's event. I was too busy pantomiming our routine over and over with Elise in the locker room.

We were in the middle of what must have been the twentieth time, when Ms. Cox came in and shouted, "Okay, we're next, girls! Let's go for it!"

Everyone jumped up. I froze.

"Come on," Elise said. "It's almost over."

I exhaled. "It hasn't even begun."

"Hey, I have an idea. If we're awful, I'll buy you an ice cream cone. If we're just mediocre, you buy me one."

I had to think about that a moment, but it

did loosen me up a tiny bit. "Elise, that's pathetic!" I exclaimed.

"But it made you smile."

"Okay, let's go," I said, getting up from my bench.

"What about the deal?"

"Sure!"

We looked at each other for a second, then gave each other a big hug and ran to the pool.

I gulped when I saw the crowd. It was standing room only! Since there were no stands at the pool complex, lots of folding chairs had been set up. But they seated only half the crowd. Off to one side, three teachers and Mr. Taylor sat at a table with clipboards and pens. They were the judges.

"Oh, boy," Elise muttered under her breath.

Ms. Cox made a brief introduction, and all of us stood by the pool and struck our poses (basically, jazz dance positions). That was part of the show, and it was good for a round of applause.

Then came the group demonstration. The music started, we all bounced for four beats, and then group one jumped in. Four beats later, our group jumped in.

First we executed some tub turns, water wheels, somersaults, and swimming strokes. Then we performed a routine of floating and moving patterns: we formed two spinning pinwheels, which became squares and then star shapes. Then we all did a final salute with one arm as we sculled to the edge of the pool. Everything happened fast, and by the end, I hadn't done any of the things I was afraid of: I hadn't sunk, I hadn't crashed into anybody, and I hadn't ended up alone at the other end of the pool.

It was a small triumph.

People seemed really impressed by the demonstration. There was a lot of "oohing" and "aahing" and applause.

"And now," Ms. Cox announced, "the most creative part of our show, the pairs competition!"

Elise and I sat with the others on a long bench, tightly holding hands. We were scheduled second.

I don't remember a thing about the first pair. My mind was going over and over our routine, step by step — until I drew a blank.

"Elise!" I whispered frantically. "What happens after the corkscrew turn?"

Elise gave me a bewildered look.

"And now," Ms. Cox announced, "Elise Coates and Jessica Ramsey!"

"Yeah, Jessi!" I could hear my father shouting.

There was no time to think. No time to wonder about the corkscrew turn. If I forgot it, I forgot it.

We walked to the edge of the pool and stood there in our Nefertiti poses. The music began.

We jumped into the water. My mind may have been blank, but my body knew just what to do. I rose above water and matched Elise stroke for stroke. We did our turns. We "planked" (a move in which one girl slips underneath her partner and comes up the other side). We executed the corkscrew turn and our Egyptian arms. We performed our ending, which involved my riding on Elise's shoulders. Then it was over.

How was it? I have no idea. How did I feel? Numb. What did people think of it? They clapped.

Elise and I took a bow, then walked off to a bench on the side. We just sat there, staring straight ahead. I don't know about Elise, but I felt as if every ounce of energy had been squeezed out of me. All this time, all this work . . . and now — poof! — it was over.

Somehow it didn't seem real.

The other pairs performed, but I don't remember much about them either. I just remember feeling glad when Mr. Taylor stepped up to the pool — because that meant we'd soon be going home.

"That concludes the swimming part of the program," he began.

Everyone cheered. Elise and I stood up. I

was beginning to feel cold and hoped to get into the locker room first.

"Except for the awards . . ." Mr. Taylor continued.

I started walking, then stopped. It would be rude not to applaud the winners.

"Starting with synchro . . . well, it was a tough decision, as you can imagine . . ."

Hurry up, I thought.

"But the winner of the gold medal for the pairs goes to . . ."

He paused dramatically. I was freezing and getting a little annoyed.

"Jessica Ramsey and Elise Coates!"

I thought he was joking. Then my eyes focused on the crowd, and I saw Mama, Daddy, and Aunt Cecelia standing and cheering. *Then* I felt myself being smothered by Elise's arms.

"We did it! We did it, Jessi!" she was screaming.

I wanted to faint. I wanted to cry. But I didn't do either. Instead I hugged Elise back, and both of us jumped up and down like little kids.

Laughing, Ms. Cox gave us a gentle push to the left. I turned around and saw Mr. Taylor standing with the contest judges, holding out two gold-colored medals.

As Elise and I walked toward them, I could barely feel my feet touching the ground.

CHAPTER 14

"Potato sacks stacked up?"

"Yessss."

"Yes *what*?"

"Yes, *ma'am*."

Alan Gray clenched his teeth. He wasn't used to taking orders — and having to say "ma'am" to Kristy was driving him crazy. It was the morning of the Mini-Olympics, and we were working hard, but Kristy's personal servant was working the hardest of all.

"Bullhorn batteries replaced?" Kristy barked.

"Yuzmumm . . ." Alan mumbled.

"What?"

"*Yes, ma'am!*"

"Good! Now go get the refreshments — on the double!"

Alan slumped toward the house.

"I said on the double!" Kristy ordered.

Alan walked a teeny bit faster — and Kristy turned to us and grinned.

"Kristy, you're *terrible!*" Claudia said with a smile.

Kristy shrugged. "Hey, he agreed to the challenge, right? Imagine what he'd have done to me if *he* had won!"

Claudia nodded. "Good point."

From inside, we could hear Mr. Spier saying, "Hi, Alan! Everything's on trays, ready to go. Want to taste-test this batch of cookies?"

"Well, at least *somebody's* being nice to him," I said.

Just then a familiar voice called out, "Hi, guys!"

I almost didn't recognize Elise in regular clothes, I was so used to seeing her in a bathing suit.

"Hi, Elise!" I said. "Come on over."

My memories of the synchro competition came rushing back. After the award ceremony, I had felt stunned. Mama and Daddy had had a barbecue afterward and had invited Elise and my BSC friends. By nighttime my cheeks had hurt from grinning so much. I went to bed two hours early and slept through my alarm the next morning.

Not till Saturday, the day of the Mini-Olympics, did I feel normal again. All that practicing had taken a lot out of me. I was glad not to have to worry about sculling and tub turns any more.

As if she were reading my mind, Elise said, "Ready to go to the pool?"

"Aaaaaagh!" I cried out. "Not the pool!"

Elise laughed. "Just kidding. How's it going here? Can I help set up?"

"No, Alan's doing it all," Claudia replied.

Alan came outside carrying two trays of cookies. There was a chocolate stain on his face — and a big grin.

"Put them down and fill the kiddie pool!" Kristy commanded.

"She's really giving it to him, huh?" Elise said.

"You bet," Stacey replied. "Hey, you guys, can you help me set up the prize table?"

"Sure," I said. Elise and I helped Stacey move a picnic table to the side, where we would be giving out ribbons to the prize winners. And since everyone was going to be a prize winner, that meant tying lots of bows, and writing labels like MOST IMPROVED, MOST DEDICATED, MOST ENTHUSIASTIC, and any other "most" we could think of.

I had brought Becca along with me, and she and Mal were putting down markers for the "sprints." Oh, by the way, Mal's ankle was healing great. In fact, she had come to our Wednesday barbecue using only a cane — and by Saturday she was limping on her own without any assistance.

It was a fast recovery, wasn't it? Sort of makes you think "Hmmm . . ."

Oh, well. At nine o'clock A.M., an hour before starting time, Charlotte arrived with a stack of papers.

Becca ran down the driveway to greet her, and Claudia called out, "The posters are here!"

Charlotte, the anti-athlete, had become the official sign maker for the Mini-Olympics. She had been inspired when Mary Anne took her suggestion about working the concession stand at the SMS Sports Festival.

Mary Anne and I followed Becca, and we helped Char fasten a sign to a lamppost:

THE
OFFICIAL SITE
OF THE
FIRST ANNUAL
BSC MINI-OLYMPICS!
10:00 A.M. TO 4:00 P.M.

At precisely 9:45, the Hobarts and the Pikes arrived (in three separate cars), and the pandemonium began.

It started when both sets of parents reached into the Hobarts' trunk to pull out four bulky canvas bags. "Where do we put the weights?" Mrs. Hobart asked.

"I guess by the garage," Mary Anne said.

"I want to practice!" said Nicky Pike, jumping up and down behind them.

"No, I want to!" said Johnny Hobart.

"I call first!" said James Hobart.

"Wait a minute, guys — " Mary Anne started to say.

"I *said* it first!" Nicky shouted.

"But you didn't *call* it!" James retorted.

"No, me!" Johnny insisted, on the verge of tears.

"Daaaad!" screamed Nicky.

"Mommmm!" screamed James.

It was fifteen minutes before starting time, and we had our first fight. It was going to be a long day.

Next to arrive were the Rodowskys. Jackie Rodowsky, who's seven, is known in the BSC as "the Walking Disaster" — and he proved his reputation right away.

In the middle of the yard, Alan and Kristy had set up a kiddie pool for "sailboat" races. Contestants (two at a time) would put a toy boat in the water at a "starting line," then blow through long plastic straws to provide the wind.

Just beyond the pool was a big maple tree with a Velcro bull's-eye for an archery contest.

Unfortunately, that was the event that caught Jackie's eye first.

"Hey, I want to be Robin Hood!" he shouted. He ran toward the target. He tripped, and . . .

Splaasssh! Guess where Jackie landed? Water splashed everywhere. Jackie cried out in surprise as he fell in facefirst.

Mrs. Rodowsky rushed to him. Kristy rushed to him. Jackie sat up, looking confused. A sailboat was sticking to his collar. He smiled and shrugged.

One good thing — Jackie had to go home and change, so we didn't have to worry about him for awhile.

In the next few minutes, Kristy's family arrived, then the Hsus, the Prezziosos, the Kormans, the Newtons, the Braddocks . . . and then I stopped counting.

At ten o'clock, Kristy blew a whistle. When everyone was quiet, she made an announcement, reading from an index card she had prepared:

"Um, we're about to begin the first annual BSC Mini-Olympics. Parent and BSC volunteers will be at each contest station throughout the day. The contest will run continuously, as long as we have enough contestants. Kids, if you see an event you want to enter, and no one is there to run it, just let one of the BSC members know. If you have to leave early, you may come back for prize announcements at four o'clock. Best of luck, everybody!"

The kids started squealing and running around. There was a shoving match at the starting line of the sprints, but Watson took care of that in his quiet way.

In a far corner, the Wiffle ball derby began. Lucky for us, Logan Bruno had arrived, and he said he'd be in charge of it all day.

At least, I thought we were lucky to have him — until he started *coaching* the kids. Now, Logan was on the SMS baseball team, so he really knows what he's doing. Before long, Wiffle balls began flying all over the place. Marilyn Arnold got bonked on the head while she was in a potato-sack race. Matt Braddock hit a home run that landed on Linny Papadakis's chest as he was bench-pressing a barbell. He gasped in surprise, his elbows buckled, and the barbell came down on his chest. Luckily Mr. Pike was spotting him and pulled the barbell up.

"He loses!" David Michael shouted with glee. "I win!"

"No fair!" Linny bellowed.

Mary Anne had a long talk with Logan, and there were many more short pop flies the rest of the afternoon.

But considering the chaos, everything went

130

surprisingly well. Supplies lasted, parents co-operated, and there was a feeling of excitement in the air — along with the Wiffle balls, soap bubbles, and surgical-glove balloons.

The kids had a blast. Most of them entered two or three contests, and some of them (like Linny) entered the same one over and over, trying to set a record each time.

Then there was Andrew Brewer. A few weeks earlier he had vowed not to be in the Mini-Olympics. But he was running around and laughing, lining up for practically every single event. He entered the archery contest, and never once hit the target. He entered a sprint and came in second to last. He entered a potato-sack race and fell flat on his face. He tried the sailboat race but couldn't blow hard enough, and gave himself a headache.

At one point I saw him snuggled in his mom's arms, sucking his thumb. My heart went out to him for trying so hard.

Kristy supervised, going from event to event. And wherever she went, her butler tagged along behind. Alan picked up stray Velcro arrows. Alan tied shoelaces. Alan cleaned up spilled food. Alan refilled the lemonade and got more cookies.

Then Jamie Newton had a little problem after a potato-sack race. It seems he had wolfed down about a hundred Oreo cookies just beforehand, and with all that jumping up and down — well, I don't need to go into graphic detail. I'll just let you guess who had cleanup duty.

All in all, Saturday was probably not on Alan Gray's list of top ten favorite days.

The hours passed by in a blur. My favorite part was seeing my sister's excitement. Becca didn't participate in anything, but she *loved* watching! All day long she ran around, wide-eyed, as if the Summer Olympics had come to town.

And that was the whole idea, wasn't it?

When four o'clock rolled around, a lot of kids were still left. By that time, the parents were moving awfully slowly. Kristy made Alan go inside and fix coffee. But judging from the looks on some of the parents' faces when they took a sip, he must not have done it right.

The last contest of the day was a "crosscountry" race. That meant two laps around the property, including the front and back yards. Suzi Barrett, Johnny Hobart, and Jenny Prezzioso had entered. Watson was standing by the finish line, looking like he couldn't wait to sit down.

Suddenly Andrew came dashing across the lawn. "Wait, Daddy!" he shouted. "I want to be in it!"

Watson smiled palely. He was probably

thinking what I was thinking — Andrew would be better off quitting before he got too upset. Still, the other kids *were* about his age (four), so maybe he'd have a good chance.

Andrew lined up next to the others.

"Okay, ready . . . ?" Watson announced. "Set . . . *go!*"

The kids dug in. Johnny got off to a fast start, but Jenny and Andrew were right behind him. Suzi was last, shouting, "Wait! Wait!"

Her brother, Buddy, slapped his forehead in big-brother disgust. "They can't *wait*! It's a *race!*" he yelled from the sidelines.

The runners disappeared behind the house, then appeared a moment later around the other side. This time, Andrew and Jenny were in the lead, neck and neck.

"Come on, Andrew!" Kristy shouted. (I wanted to shout, too, but it wouldn't have been right. *I'm* not his sister.)

They made the turn for the second lap. Andrew was pulling in the lead. His face was red, and he was huffing and puffing.

By the last lap, Andrew was in third place. He hadn't paced himself, and he was gasping for breath. And that was how he crossed the finish line, only a couple of steps ahead of Suzi.

Lucky for him, Watson was waiting there with open arms, ready to pick up his sobbing son who had tried and tried till the end.

CHAPTER 15

"*Pssssst!* Go ahead, press it *now!*" Kristy said in a loud whisper.

Alan scowled. He was standing next to Dawn's tape recorder, which was plugged into an outdoor electrical outlet on the wall of the house. Obeying Kristy, he pressed play.

A loud trumpet fanfare echoed through the backyard. "Hear ye! Hear ye!" Kristy announced through her bullhorn in a grand voice. "We have reached the conclusion of the First Annual Mini-Olympics. Gather around for the official awarding of prizes!"

The trumpet fanfare had turned into this raucous brass number, with trombones and tubas blatting away. Kristy put down the bullhorn and hissed at Alan, "That's *enough!* Press *stop!*"

Alan let it go a few seconds longer. When he did turn it off, this tiny smile was on his face.

"Thank you . . . *maestro*," Kristy said in her announcer voice again. "May I have the basket, please?"

The rest of us BSCers were next to the table, holding a wicker wastebasket full of ribbons. It was 4:17, and we had just spent the most frantic seventeen minutes of our lives filling in names on the prizes, making sure everyone received one.

Stacey held up the basket and Kristy picked out a ribbon. "I shall now present the first award!" With a dramatic flourish, she lifted it up and read the tag. "And the Most Creative Award is hereby . . . uh, *awarded* to . . ." Kristy cleared her throat. "Charlotte Johanssen!"

And "Merriment spread throughout the Land." (That's from an old fairy tale I read. It's a fancy way of saying, "Everybody clapped.")

I heard Stacey whisper to Kristy, "Uh, could you step it up? There are a lot more in the basket."

Kristy pulled out the second one and read, "The Crosscountry Champ . . . Johnny Hobart!"

Johnny ran forward, and I caught a glimpse of Andrew's face, pouty and sad, probably thinking of the race he had almost won.

Most Frequent Weight-Lifting Award . . .

Linny Papadakis!" Kristy announced next.

As the crowd cheered, Linny's face lit up like a lantern. You'd think he had won an Oscar or something. He grabbed his ribbon and held it triumphantly in the air.

Kristy picked another. "The Most Determined Award . . ." She paused. Her solemn "announcer" expression melted into a warm smile. "This is a very special one, and it goes to Andrew Brewer!"

Andrew's mouth just dropped open. He looked around in disbelief at all the people smiling and cheering. Mrs. Brewer hugged him, then gave him a gentle push forward.

I could hear him say "thank you" in a teeny voice as he took the ribbon from his stepsister.

The award ceremony left everyone feeling happy. We managed to give all the kids something, right on down to Most Summery Outfit or Smoothest Running Style. (We were really stretching it.)

By five o'clock the last of the families had drifted off. Elise thanked me for inviting her, and my parents asked her over for dinner the next week. We both agreed to buy each other ice cream cones afterward, since we both lost our bet.

That left all us BSC members to clean up. Well, I should say all of us minus one. Kristy was lounging on a lawn chair, sipping iced tea.

Her butler had taken her place.

"More, please," Kristy said, handing her empty glass to Alan. As he went inside, grumbling, she said, "You know, I'm really proud of my stepbrother. He never gave up trying, the whole day long."

"If he keeps that up, he can't help but be a winner," I said. Boy, that sounded corny, but I really believed it. My synchro experience had taught me that.

Dawn nodded in agreement. "You know, they're just *kids*, but sometimes you can really learn things from them."

"Yeah," Mary Anne said. "Like Charlotte. I never imagined she'd figure out how to get both us nonjocks involved in these jock events."

Mallory sighed. She had this strange, pinched look on her face, like she was dying to say something. "I — I guess I should have talked to Char."

"What do you mean?" I asked.

"Well . . ." Mal said, "if I had, maybe I wouldn't have tried to chicken out like I did."

"But you sprained your ankle," Kristy said. "That's not chickening out."

Suddenly Claudia gave Mal a look. "You didn't sprain it on *purpose*, did you — in that potato-sack race?"

"Yes—I mean, no," Mal said uncomfortably. "I mean, I wanted to *pretend* to hurt myself. I figured if everyone believed me, then I wouldn't have to be in the festival. But I guess I was trying too hard. A real sprain wasn't in the plan." She sighed. "Then I stayed on crutches longer than I needed to, so no one would bother me about joining in at the last minute."

"Mal," I said gently, "maybe if you'd just admitted from the beginning that you didn't want to be in the festival, you wouldn't have had to go through all that."

"Yeah," Mal said quietly. "I know."

No one knew what to say for a moment, so I broke the ice. "Well, we all make mistakes. Elise and I decided synchro class wasn't for us. We're not returning."

"*What?*" Stacey said. "But you're so good at it — and you worked so hard."

I nodded. "Synchro's a great sport, and I can see why people like it. But for Elise and me, it was, like, too much work and too little *fun*. She told me she was starting to mess up in her regular swim class, which she loves. And I realized I didn't have enough energy for ballet. So when we looked at it that way, the decision to quit was easy."

Slam!

The back door flew open and shut as Alan

stalked out, carrying another iced tea. Kristy took one look at the glass and said, "Where's the lemon?"

And that was when it happened. Alan's neck tightened up, his eyes reddened, and he looked like he was either going to explode or cry.

The rest of us scattered, picking up odds and ends around the yard.

Alan smacked Kristy's drink down on the table. Iced tea splattered all over his pants, but he didn't seem to notice. "Okay!" he said, practically spitting the word out. "I'll get you your stupid lemon. I'll get you whatever you want, Kristy. But I challenge you to another race — just you and me, without all your friends around. And this one'll be for *two* weeks of personal service."

Kristy stared at him. I think she was a little shocked.

"What do you say to that, *ma'am*?" Alan said sarcastically.

Kristy slowly lifted the iced tea to her lips. Before she took a sip, she smiled at Alan and said, "You're on. Now go change your pants."

Alan looked down at the brown iced-tea stain that was spreading down his leg. He opened his mouth. Then he shut it. No words came out.

As for me, I held my breath. I vowed I'd pass out before I allowed myself to laugh. To my left, I saw Mary Anne's shoulders start to shake. To my right, I saw Mallory put her hand over her mouth.

My vow lasted about two seconds. I burst out giggling. Soon the yard echoed with laughter — mine, Mal's, Kristy's, Mary Anne's, Dawn's, Stacey's, Claud's.

And finally, Alan's, too.